He knew he couldn't just grab her dad's records away from her and leave. As much as he dreaded having to offer her comfort, and knowing what it was going to do to him to be that close to her, he was all she had.

She made a face. "I don't like to cry. It just messes up my face and gives me a headache."

She met his gaze and he marveled at how blue her eyes were. He'd thought from the beginning that they were lovely. "I think you have the most beautiful eyes I've ever seen."

He had a sudden need to swallow—hard. Here they went again. Just like before, he sat perfectly still and hoped like hell that she didn't kiss him, because he was already very much on the edge.

She's your responsibility. Your responsibility.

He leaned forward, his gaze moving from her eyes to her lips. Then, as she let her eyes drift shut, he brushed her mouth with his.

Dirty
Little Secrets

MALLORY KANE

First published in Great Britain 2013
by Mills & Boon, an imprint of Harlequin (UK) Limited.
Large Print edition 2013
Harlequin (UK) Limited,
Eton House, 18-24 Paradise Road,
Richmond, Surrey TW9 1SR

© Rickey R. Mallory 2013

ISBN: 978 0 263 23826 6

Harlequin (UK) policy is to use papers that are natural, renewable and recyclable products and made from wood grown in sustainable forests. The logging and manufacturing process conform to the legal environmental regulations of the country of origin.

Printed and bound in Great Britain
by CPI Antony Rowe, Chippenham, Wiltshire

MALLORY KANE

has two very good reasons for loving reading and writing. Her mother was a librarian, who taught her to love and respect books as a precious resource. Her father could hold listeners spellbound for hours with his stories. He was always her biggest fan.

She loves romantic suspense with dangerous heroes and dauntless heroines, and enjoys tossing in a bit of her medical knowledge for an extra dose of intrigue. After twenty-five books published, Mallory is still amazed and thrilled that she actually gets to make up stories for a living.

Mallory lives in Tennessee with her computer-genius husband and three exceptionally intelligent cats. She enjoys hearing from readers. You can write her at mallory@mallorykane.com or via Mills & Boon.

For Michael:
Hang in there, baby. I love you.

Chapter One

Everything had been planned—from every lock that had to be picked, to every step through every corridor. The Louis Royale Hotel's popular restaurants had cleared out by midnight and most of the diners had moved on to more exciting places or gone home. The hotel's bar was popular for lunch and predinner cocktails, but most serious partiers ended up on Bourbon Street by late evening.

It had been simple to slip in with the last of the late diners. Simple to take the elevators up to the tenth floor. And it was a snap to pick the lock on the fire stairs door to the penthouse suite that took up the entire eleventh floor. The hotel still used the original ornate metal keys, although the guest rooms also had computerized security card locks.

The hotel was the perfect place to kill the senator. And tonight was the perfect night. His offices and the senate floor in Baton Rouge were too public and too secure. The locked gates of his home just outside of that city put the Louisiana State Legislature's security measures to shame. It was laughable that the man who'd erected a fortress worthy of a paranoid potentate was so lax about his safety in a hotel. But then, a lot of people assumed a hotel's penthouse suite was innately secure. Tonight, for Senator Darby Sills, that assumption would prove to be a fatal mistake.

Crouching in the fire stairs to wait for the perfect moment was also a snap. Boring, cramped, but simple. The layout of the penthouse suite was perfect. The elevator doors opened into the sitting room. On the left wall were the double doors to the master suite and on the right was the door to a second, smaller bedroom.

It was after midnight, one twenty-seven, to be specific. The senator and his staff were due to have breakfast with the local longshore-men's union at eight o'clock in the morning. He'd probably sent his staff off to their rooms by eleven, eleven-thirty at the latest. Sills insisted that his employees maintain a routine. He liked to say that any man or woman worth their salt should be in bed by eleven and up by seven. Not that Senator Sills abided by that rule. No one in public life could maintain a healthy, structured sleep schedule.

Although few people were aware of it, Sills was an insomniac. He rarely got four hours' sleep a night. At home, he'd sit in a rocking chair in his study, smoke his pipe, sip Dewar's scotch and read. It was widely rumored that his staff had the unenviable task of keeping the senator and his scotch separated when he was on the road.

The plan to kill Senator Sills allowed seven minutes for the job, start to finish. Best scenario, Sills would be in the sitting room, reading. A quick entrance through the service door, a muffled shot, right in the middle of Sills's chest, a rapid escape and down the fire stairs. If Sills had already retired to the bedroom, seven minutes would be stretching it, but it could still be done.

Next, change to the clothes hidden in the fire stairs while descending to the first floor, then walk through the bar and out the door as if nothing was more important than heading left toward Bourbon Street. Seven minutes, one bullet, and the greedy bastard would be dead.

LANEY MONTGOMERY CLOSED the connecting door between the penthouse suite sitting room and the adjoining bedroom with an exhausted sigh. She'd thought the senator would never stop editing his speech. He was pickier than usual tonight.

She kicked off her heels and collapsed on the king-size bed, too tired to lift her arm to check her watch. The last time she'd checked, it had been after two, and she had to get up at six to make any final changes to Louisiana State Senator Darby Sills's speech before his eight o'clock breakfast meeting with the local officers of the Longshoremen's Association.

But as much as she wanted to just turn over, grab a corner of the bedspread for warmth and drift off to sleep, she couldn't. She had to brush her teeth, take off her makeup and set her phone's alarm first. She felt around for her phone, then remembered that she'd left it on the printer cart in the sitting room.

With a weary sigh, she sat up. For a brief moment she fantasized about leaving the phone where it was and calling for a wakeup call, but she couldn't spend three hours—not even three hours while she was asleep—without her phone. As Senator Darby Sills's personal assistant, she'd be the one called if anything happened. Whether it was a change in the number of people attending the longshoremen's breakfast or a frantic text from the governor about some issue facing the legislature, it came to her phone.

She closed her eyes. Maybe nobody would call tonight. And surely she'd hear her phone through the door. Just as she began to sink into the soft bed, she heard a loud yet muffled pop through the connecting door, then a thud. Was that pop a bottle being uncorked? Had the senator smuggled in a bottle of scotch?

Ready with her "remember what the doctor said about your liver" speech, she vaulted up and knocked briskly. "Senator? I forgot my phone," she called, then opened the door and stepped through.

The desk chair where Senator Sills had been sitting just two minutes before was empty. Laney glanced toward the wet bar. The senator liked his Dewar's on the rocks. "Senator," she called. "Where did you get—?"

Then she saw the scarecrow-thin shadow looming in front of her.

Laney's hands shot up in an instinctive protective gesture. "What? Senator—?"

The shadow took on a vaguely human outline—a silhouette completely cloaked in black. It came toward her and she recoiled. "Who are you?" she cried. "Where's the senator?"

The person in black lifted its right arm and pointed at her.

Laney blinked and tried to clear her vision. Surely there was something wrong with her eyes. "Senator—" she started, but stopped when something in the person's hand caught the lamplight, gleaming like silver.

"No!" she cried, her subconscious mind recognizing the object before her brain had time to attach a name to it. She dived, face-planting on the hardwood floor in front of her bedroom door. A muffled pop echoed through the room and her skull burned in white-hot pain. Her head was knocked back into the baseboard behind her. Her cry choked and died as her throat seized in fear.

What happened? What hurt so bad? Again, her brain was slow to catch up to her intuitive subconscious. Finally she understood. *I've been shot.* Whimpering involuntarily, she drew her shoulders up and pressed her forehead into the floorboards as hard as she could. She wrapped her arms around her head, grimacing in awful anticipation as she waited for the next bullet to slam into her.

And waited. There were no more pops. Instead, she heard footsteps coming toward her. They echoed hollowly on the hardwood floor.

One step. Two. She thought about moving. Pictured herself propelling backward through the door to her room and slamming it. But it didn't matter how brave she was inside her head. In reality, she couldn't make her frozen limbs move. All she could do was cower.

Three steps. He was coming to check and be sure she was dead. He was going to shoot her again, at point-blank range. She didn't want to die. "No—" she croaked. "Please—"

The elevator bell dinged.

The footsteps stopped. The man whispered a

curse. Laney held her breath. Who was on the elevator? Who would have access to the penthouse? Had someone heard the shots?

The footsteps sounded again, but this time they were quicker and fading, as if the man were retreating. Laney opened her eyes to slits, bracing for the sharp, nauseating pain. She had to know where the man was—what he was doing.

When she raised her head, a moan escaped her lips. The shooter whirled and something silvery and bright caught the light again. He was holding the gun at shoulder height, pointed right at her. She gasped and tried to shrink into the floor. At that instant the distinctive sound of elevator doors opening filled the air.

The man turned as if to glance over his shoulder, then disappeared through the service door to the left of the elevators. His footsteps echoed, warring with the electronic sound of the doors.

With a massive effort, Laney lifted her head. Coming out of the elevator was a bellman carrying a bottle of Dewar's scotch. She pointed with a trembling finger toward the service door and cried out, "Help. He's getting away!" Only it wasn't a cry. It was nothing more than a choked whisper.

The bellman saw her then. He dropped the bottle, which thudded to the floor without breaking. "Oh, God!" he cried, running over to kneel beside her. "Oh, God. Are you all right? What happened? Where are you hurt?"

"Senator—" Laney forced herself to say. She pointed toward the desk. "The senator—"

The young man twisted to look in the direction she was pointing. "Oh, God," he said again.

"Help him," she whispered.

"I can't—" the bellman started. "The blood—"

Laney pushed herself to her knees. "Senator!" she cried out as she crawled toward the empty desk chair, hoping against hope that the gunman hadn't killed him. That somehow the shot had missed him and he had taken shelter under the desk, wounded maybe, but alive. As she crawled closer, she saw his back. He was lying next to the chair, crumpled into a fetal position. Blood made a glistening, widening stain on the Persian rug.

"Senator!" she cried again, shoving the chair out of the way. Twisting, she pinned the bellman with a glare that ratcheted up the throbbing pain in her head. "Call the police," she grated.

She put her hand on the senator's shoulder and carefully turned him onto his back—and saw his eyes, open and staring and beginning to film over.

"Oh, no," she whispered. "No, no, no." She shook him by the shoulder. His jacket fell open and she saw where the blood was coming from. A small, seeping wound in his chest. She cast about for something to stanch the bleeding, even though she knew it was too late. She looked back at his eyes and her heart sank with a dread certainty. There was no need to stop the bleeding. He was dead.

Behind her she heard the young man on the house telephone beside the elevator. "Hurry!" he said shakily. "There's blood everywhere."

Laney knew she ought to be the one on the phone, calling the police, taking care that no one but them knew what had happened. Senator Sills was dead and it was her responsibility to him and to the legislature to keep that information away from the press and the public. But her head hurt so badly and her vision was obscured by a red haze. Defeated by pain and sadness, she curled up on the floor next to the senator, one arm under her head.

Behind her, the bellman spoke into the phone. "No. I'm telling you, it's Senator Sills. I think he's dead."

NEW ORLEANS POLICE Detective Ethan Delancey stared down at the body of Senator Darby Sills, sprawled on the floor of the penthouse suite in the Louis Royale Hotel in the French Quarter. Blood stained the Persian rug beneath him. This was going to be ugly.

"This is going to be ugly," Detective Dixon Lloyd's voice came from behind him.

"Morning, partner," Ethan responded wryly. "Nice of you to show up." He'd gotten to the hotel fifteen minutes earlier. But then he didn't have a wife or a house in the lower Garden District like Dixon did. His apartment on Prytania Street was less than ten minutes from the

French Quarter in rush hour, much less at four o'clock in the morning.

"Hey, give me a break," Dixon said. "Did you see how many reporters are already outside? Not to mention rubberneckers. I had to call the commander to round up more officers for crowd control."

"Everybody in New Orleans will know Senator Sills is dead before the sun comes up," Ethan said glumly.

"Probably already do. I hate politics."

"You?" Ethan countered. "Try being Con Delancey's grandson." Like his older brother Lucas and his twin cousins, Ryker and Reilly, Ethan had become a cop, hoping to separate himself from the tarnished legacy of his infamous grandfather, Louisiana Senator Con Delancey. But like them, he'd quickly found out that the name Delancey was an occupational hazard in New Orleans, no matter what

the job was. There was nowhere in the state of Louisiana—or maybe the world—that his surname didn't evoke a raised eyebrow and a range of reactions from an appreciative smile to unbridled hostility.

"I think I can relate," Dixon said, "since I'm in the family now."

"You two finished catching up on family gossip?" Police Officer Maria Farrantino interrupted. "I'm sure it's been a couple of hours since you've seen each other." She stood on the other side of the body, the toes of her polished boots avoiding the pool of blood by less than two inches.

Ethan sent her an irritated glare.

Unfazed, she continued. "I've got the second victim over here. The first officer on the scene took her statement. The EMTs are working on her now, and CSI hasn't gotten to her yet."

Ethan looked at the young woman who was

sitting on a straight-backed chair with her head bowed and one hand holding back her dark, matted hair as an EMT applied a bandage to the side of her head. Draped over her knee was a wet cloth that was stained a deep pink, the same color as the large spot on her white shirt. According to the statement the first officer had given him, she was Senator Sills's personal assistant and had surprised the killer in the act. She'd told the officer that she'd dived to the floor when the killer had turned his gun on her, but hadn't been quick enough to escape injury.

Ethan's gaze slid downward to the short black skirt that had ridden up to reveal a pair of class A legs ending in bare feet.

"Yo, Delancey," Dixon said and waved a hand across his field of vision. Ethan blinked and turned his head.

"What?"

"Ah, you're back to earth," Dixon said. "Have you talked to the medical examiner yet?"

Ethan shook his head.

"Your choice. The M.E. or the injured victim with the killer legs that go on forever?"

"Legs. No question," Ethan muttered.

Dixon winked at Ethan as he headed toward the man bending over the senator's body.

"What's her name?" Ethan asked Farrantino as he squinted at the scribbled words on the officer's statement. He was going to have to ask that the officers receive penmanship lessons.

"Let's see. Montgomery. Elaine," Farrantino answered.

Montgomery. His gaze snapped back to the witness just as the EMT finished with the bandage and she raised her head. He took in her features for the first time. Could her name be a coincidence? With a sinking feeling in the pit of his stomach, he thought about the late, infamous lobbyist Elliott Montgomery, comparing his memory of Montgomery's narrow features and dark blue eyes to Elaine Montgomery's face. It didn't take much imagination to see the resemblance. The slender nose, full mouth and high cheekbones looked a lot better on her than they had on him, though.

So, Senator Darby Sills's personal assistant was the daughter of the ruthless lobbyist for the Port of New Orleans unions. Ethan frowned. Was this case about to get even uglier? "Looks like the EMTs are done with her. What about the crime scene techs?"

Farrantino glanced toward the two young men in CSI jackets. "It's probably going to be another five minutes or so before they can get to her."

"Fine," he said. "I'll see how far I can get." He stepped up to her with a small spiral notepad in his hand. "I'm Detective Ethan Delancey. I hope you feel up to talking for a bit, because I need to ask you a few questions. You are—?"

"I'm—Elaine Montgomery. Laney."

"Okay, Ms. Montgomery. Can you tell me what happened here? Briefly?"

She had closed her eyes and was touching the area around the bandage the EMTs had applied with her fingertips. "What?"

"What happened?" he repeated.

"A man shot Senator Sills and when I walked in, he sh-shot me."

"Did you see the man shoot the senator?"

Her face seemed to crumple a bit. "No."

"Where was Senator Sills? Was he still alive?" Ethan had barely gotten the question out when Farrantino gestured to him.

He excused himself and walked over to the officer, who handed him a cell phone. "Sills's," she said. "You might be interested in some of his recent calls."

Ethan checked the phone's incoming call log. "'Senator Myron Stamps,'" he read. Then a little farther down, "'The U.S. federal minimum-security prison at Oakdale, Louisiana.'" He looked up at Farrantino. "That's where Congressman Gavin Whitley is. Here." He handed the phone back to her. "Take this and retrieve all the calls and times and the texts as well as voice mails."

"How far back?" Farrantino asked.

"Far as it goes," Ethan said. "Get me the list. We might want to talk with all of them. And set up an interview with Whitley and Stamps *this* morning. I want to find out why they were calling Sills."

"Are you thinking this has something to do with Kate Chalmet's son's kidnapping?"

Ethan thought about his brother Travis, who'd come home to New Orleans eight months before, to find out that he had a son and that the four-year-old had been kidnapped. "Could be. Whitley claimed that it was Sills's money that paid for the kidnapper."

"I remember," Farrantino said, then nodded toward Elaine Montgomery. "The crime scene techs are ready for her."

"What do the EMTs say?" he asked.

"They want her checked out at the E.R. just in case. They think the wound is superficial, but they want a CT scan to rule out internal bleeding."

"Okay. As soon as I'm done here, I'm going by the E.R. to see if I can get in a few more questions. Otherwise it's going to be hours before I can finish with Whitley and Stamps and talk to her again."

As Farrantino gave him a nod and headed toward Laney Montgomery, Ethan's partner returned to his side. "Okay," Dixon said. "We've got a preliminary time of death. The M.E. said he's been dead two, maybe three hours at the most."

"Great. The hotel's been cordoned off and everyone is being questioned. Thankfully there are no conventions or weddings scheduled for today. The only event is—or was—the longshoremen's breakfast, where the senator was scheduled to speak."

"Yeah. Still, I doubt our murderer has been hanging around for hours waiting to see if we can pick him out of a crowd," Dixon said wryly.

"Farrantino is bringing in Myron Stamps for questioning, and arranging with the warden at Oakdale to question Gavin Whitley," Ethan said. "Both of them called Sills within the last couple of days. I want to know exactly where Stamps is now and where he was all evening. And I'm going to get every single phone call and every visitor Whitley has had since he went inside." He didn't have to tell Dixon why he wanted to talk to them.

Dixon nodded. "It must have really rankled to be under indictment like Whitley or facing certain loss in the next election like Stamps, and know that Sills came out of the kidnapping scandal smelling like a rose. I'd be surprised if both of them hadn't wanted to kill Sills. But do you think Whitley could have arranged this from prison?"

"No. I don't think he has the connections or the cojones to set up something like that at all, much less handle it from prison. But we'd better check it out." The two of them stepped aside as the body of Senator Darby Sills was rolled out the door.

"Okay," Ethan said. "I'm going by the hospital to talk with Elaine Montgomery, because I'm probably going to be tied up all morning with those two."

"You know we've got to bring Travis in."

Ethan grimaced. He sure as hell didn't want to make his older brother come in for questioning, especially after everything Travis had been through in the past months. He'd like to give Travis and Kate and their son, Max, time to recover and heal from Travis's months as a hostage and Max's kidnapping ordeal. They needed time to get used to being together, to being a family.

"I know," Ethan said dejectedly. "I'm sure I'll be hearing from the D.A. within the next hour or two, making sure I've questioned him as a person of interest in Sills's death, despite the fact that there was no evidence connecting Sills with the kidnapping. I'll call him in a little while." He looked at his watch. "He'll be up and out on a run by six. Maybe I can be done with him before Farrantino gets Whitley and Stamps set up."

WHEN ETHAN GOT to the emergency room and flashed his badge in order to get in to see Laney Montgomery, he found her lying on a gurney in cubicle three with a bandage on her temple, looking miserable. As he peered in, he saw her wipe her eyes with her fingertips. He stepped in through the curtain. "Hi," he said. "How's your head?"

"Who are you?" she said, sniffling.

"I'm Detective Ethan Delancey. I talked with you for a few minutes at the crime scene."

"Oh, right." She lifted her hand to touch the edges of the bandage. "I'm sorry. This has just been so—" Her voice cracked and her face crumpled. She covered her mouth with her hand.

"Hey," Ethan said, glancing behind him at the closed curtain. He didn't want the nurses to think he'd made her cry, and he sure didn't want her to get so upset that she couldn't talk.

He stepped closer to the bed. "You've been through a lot. But everything's going to be okay."

"No it's not." She looked up at the ceiling. "Senator Sills is dead. I had just left him, not five minutes before. I should have—"

Ethan waited, but she bit her lip and didn't continue. "Should have what?" he asked.

She spread her hands helplessly. "I don't know. Been there? Done something?" Her voice was rising in pitch.

He laid his hand on her arm and squeezed reassuringly, then realized what he'd done and snatched it away. "You couldn't have done anything. Not against a gun. If you'd tried, you'd probably be dead now, too.

"What we have to do now is try to catch the person who killed him and bring him to justice."

Laney cut her eyes over to him. "You can

catch him, can't you?" she said, as if she were saying *you can leap tall buildings and stop a bullet with your hand, can't you?*

He felt as though he were letting her down just by being human. He smiled at her. "I'm going to do my best," he said. "But to do that, I need to ask you some questions. Do you think you can answer them for me?"

She stared into his eyes. "Yes," she said. "Yes I can."

"Great," he said, reaching out and patting her hand. "You said you'd just left the senator. Where did you go?"

"I went to my room. I was staying in the second bedroom of the penthouse suite. When I went back into the sitting room to check on the senator after I heard the pop, he wasn't sitting in the desk chair. Before I could look for him, I saw the man dressed in black. He spotted me, he lifted his gun and I dived to the floor."

"Was the senator dead or alive at that point?"

She shook her head despairingly. "I don't know. I wasn't able to get to him until the elevator came and the shooter ran out." Her eyes glittered with tears and her hand kept darting up to her temple and stopping a fraction of an inch above the bandage. "Do you think he was lying there alive? Do you think if I'd gotten to him earlier—?"

"You can't worry about that. You were in danger. If you'd tried to get to him, the man could've gotten off a better shot. You could be dead, too. Plus, as good as the technology is, there's no way to pinpoint the second when he died. So let's take it one step at a time. You came in. The figure in black saw you, shot at you. You dived to the floor. How far away was he?"

"I don't know. Ten feet or so?" She closed her eyes. "Why are you asking me all these questions? I told the first officer all this and he wrote it down."

"Why do you think the shooter missed you?"

She frowned. "He didn't miss."

"He barely grazed your temple."

Laney peered at him sidelong. "Maybe he didn't expect me to drop to the floor."

He gave her a little smile. "Did he fire a second time?"

"No, but then you know that. You've got your CSI people and you've got the gun, don't you? And all the bullets are in the wall or the floor?"

"That's right. But he could have fired into a sofa or a pillow or something. So you only heard two—"

The nurse came in, followed by an older man dressed in blue scrubs.

"All right, Ms. Montgomery," the nurse said. "We're going to take you to get a CT scan. It won't take long, but the doctor wants to be sure you don't have an injury inside your brain that could cause bleeding."

"After they finish, I can go home, right?" Laney directed the question to Ethan. Her blue eyes pleaded with him.

"No. I'm afraid not," Ethan said. "One of the officers will take you to the police station as soon as the hospital releases you." He caught himself before he asked her if there was someone she'd like to call. That was a reflexive statement he used with witnesses all the time.

He hadn't been here ten minutes and he'd made a serious mistake. He'd been way too nice to her—way too sympathetic. He needed to start asking the tough questions. Because he didn't know what had happened in that suite yet. For the moment, Elaine Montgomery was playing three roles in this murder case—witness, victim and possible suspect.

MORE THAN FOUR hours later, Ethan looked through a two-way mirror at Laney Montgomery. She looked sad and miserable and bored. He couldn't blame her. He'd left her at the E.R. at around six o'clock, which meant she'd been here at the police station, waiting for him, for four hours. Her face and neck still weren't completely clean of blood, and a small dark spot on the bandage told him the graze on her temple was still bleeding a little. He had the EMT's report and he'd just printed out the E.R. doctor's assessment of her and the results of the CT scan. Her injury was minor. It was going to be painful for a few days, but there was no internal bleeding or damage.

As if she'd read his thoughts, she lifted her gaze to the mirror and glared at him. Or that's the impression he had. It felt as though she was staring right into his eyes, although he knew she couldn't see him through the two-way mirror. She knew he was there, though. He could see it in her suspicious gaze. He glanced away as if they'd held each other's gazes too long.

She closed her eyes and rubbed her temple gingerly, just below the edge of the bandage. Her expression changed to a wince. She looked at her fingernails, then began picking at one with a thumbnail. Even from this far away, Ethan could see the tiny leftover stains from the fingerprint ink.

He ran a hand over his face, feeling the day's growth of beard. He'd been running ever since he'd gotten the call at four o'clock this morning. By the time he'd gotten back to the station from the hotel, Travis was there, waiting to be interviewed. Then he'd taken a few minutes to review the reports from the crime scene unit, the first officer on the scene and the medical examiner, before spending almost an hour bringing Commander Jeff Wharton up to speed. He and Dixon had just finished questioning Myron Stamps and Gavin Whitley, a process that had taken over two hours, not a pleasant experience. Stamps had shown up with his lawyer. The phone call with Whitley had been a three-way, involving his attorney. Ethan's jaw ached from gritting his teeth while nearly every question he or Dixon asked was parried by their shysters.

As Dixon came into the viewing room, Laney yawned. She covered her mouth with her hand, even though there was no one in the room with her. Then she winced and patted the bandage with her fingertips again.

"She's had a long night," Dixon commented.

"She's not the only one," Ethan said, suppressing a yawn of his own. "Where'd you run off to?"

"I ran down to the lab to see what the crime

scene techs found outside the penthouse service door and on the stairs."

"What'd they find?"

Dixon pulled out a notepad. "Black scuff
marks, probably made by leather- or synthetic-
soled shoes. Not rubber. A few fibers of black
fleece, like from a sweatshirt or hoodie. That's
about it. No indication of how long they might
have been there."

"Fingerprints?"

"They dusted the service door's handle and
the railing at the top of the fire stairs, but didn't
get anything except some smudges that probably came from the shooter's gloves. There was
gunshot residue in the smudges."

"That's something, I guess."

Dixon shrugged. "They're not finished with
the penthouse suite or Laney Montgomery's
room yet, but there's nothing conclusive."

Ethan turned to look at him. "Anything on the gun or bullets?"

He nodded. "The gun is untraceable—big surprise. The bullets were fired from the gun that was found at the scene. The partial print on the gun barrel hasn't been through the system yet."

"What did you think about Whitley and Stamps?"

"I think they're telling the truth, at least about where they were last night," Dixon said.

"You know, Stamps is kind of pitiful, isn't he? I mean his wife's dead, and they never had any children. Apparently he's got no one except a housekeeper."

Dixon nodded. "It's hard not to believe him, isn't it? Home by himself. Can't say whether his housekeeper can vouch for him because she went to bed early with a headache."

"Yeah," Ethan agreed. "That was either a sad

but honest accounting of his lonely evening at home or a truly clever way to avoid having to depend on someone lying for him. The house-keeper went to bed early, therefore she can't say if he was there or not."

"I think I do believe him. He seems as though the kidnapping and his trial have taken all the starch out of him."

"And I guess Whitley's alibi is solid," Ethan said wryly, his eyes on Laney as she uncrossed her legs, recrossed them and pulled her rain-coat more tightly around her.

"I don't like him a bit—and that goes double for his lawyer."

"Pretty slick, aren't they?" Ethan sighed. "But unless Whitley got his attorney to come over here and pop Sills, I'm not sure how he could be involved. At least we know he was where he says he was."

"I wouldn't believe Whitley if he told me his

name was Whitley," Dixon said. "But no matter what I think, those alibis are good. Still, that doesn't mean one or both of them couldn't have hired someone."

"Stamps doesn't have any money—or at least none we know about. And like I said, I can't see Whitley." He thought about something. "Who went through their financial records during the kidnapping case?"

"No idea, but I'm going to check," Dixon said. "Seems like I heard that Whitley had a couple of big deposits and payouts that matched the time frame of the kidnapping. That's when Whitley tried to implicate Sills, but the forensic accountants couldn't find any proof of where the money came from."

"The amounts matched exactly the amount of money that Bentley Woods deposited in Chicago. With all Whitley's whining about Sills, I'll bet the senator's records were subpoenaed, too," Dixon responded. "No sense reinventing the wheel, if they're already there in the case file."

"Good point. You want to check on that?" Ethan asked.

"Yep. And you're going to tackle Elaine Montgomery," Dixon said, not a question.

Ethan nodded toward the glass. "I'm going to find out what she's holding back."

"Holding back?" Dixon asked him. "What do you think she's holding back on?"

"I don't know, but I can see it in her eyes. She's hiding something."

"You can see it in her eyes," Dixon said, his voice sounding choked, as if he were trying to suppress a laugh. "Those big blue ones?"

"Bite me," Ethan muttered.

"Come on Delancey. You've seen her for what, maybe ten minutes total, and now you can read her mind?" He paused before continuing. "Or maybe it's not her mind you're interested in. Last night you were all about her legs."

"Don't be crass. She's our only witness *and* she's a victim. Look at her." Ethan gestured toward the glass as Laney wet her lips, then clamped a hand tightly over her mouth as if she were holding back tears or a scream as she stared into space. "There's something on her mind and it's not just the murder of her boss."

"She looks nervous, but lots of people are terrified of being questioned by the police."

"Nope. She's hiding something," Ethan muttered, his gaze still on her. After a moment, he said to Dixon, "So what are you up to now?"

"You don't want to double-team her like we did Whitley and Stamps?" Dixon pressed.

"No," Ethan said with exaggerated patience. "I think I can handle her alone."

"Okay, if you're sure. One thing I'm going

to do is check with the CSI folks about what they've pulled from the hotel room. I'm afraid we're not going to have much, if all the guy did was sneak in, pop the senator, try to take her out, then hightail it out of there. We'll probably be lucky to get anything other than what was found on the fire stairs. Then I'll get started on pulling the Chalmet kidnapping file and see what they got on Sills."

"Okay. I'll talk to you later then."

"Watch yourself in there," Dixon said as he left.

Ethan stepped out of the viewing room and into the interview room.

Laney Montgomery looked up from inspecting her fingernails. "You know, I was printed when I started work for Senator Sills," she said, holding up her hands, palms out. "I tried to tell them but nobody would listen to me."

Ethan sat down without speaking.

"In case you're not familiar with state government policy," she went on, "employees of any public official are required to be fingerprinted. My prints are on file, here and with the FBI."

Ethan picked up one of the folders he'd brought into the room with him and paged through it. "According to the information I have, you're not a government employee. You're an independent contractor working directly for Senator Sills."

"I still had to declare my allegiance to the United States and to Louisiana and be fingerprinted and photographed before I could go to work for him. About thirty seconds of listening to me could have saved the police department about a pint of ink," she finished drily.

Ethan looked back at the page in front of him, waiting to see what she would say next.

She glanced around the room, then looked at

the mirror. "Is everyone else staying in there to watch?" she asked, nodding toward the mirror.

"In there?" Ethan asked.

The look she sent him was equal parts disgust and irritation. A "you don't think I'm that dumb, do you?" expression. "The room behind the mirror."

"Nobody's in there now," he said as he sat down in a wooden straight-backed chair and tipped it backward onto two legs. He watched her.

She sat silent for a few moments, casting about for something to settle her gaze on, then she looked directly at him. "What?" she said.

He raised his eyebrows.

"Stop trying to make me say something by being silent."

He lowered the front legs of the chair to the floor. He liked that she wasn't easily rattled. But he wasn't fooled by her outburst. She'd turned a favorite tactic of his back onto him. Break a silence with a noncommittal comment or an attack on the other person. But he knew how to play this game. "Okay. I'll stop being quiet. Is there something you want to tell me?"

Her gaze stayed on his face and her mouth turned up slightly. "No. Is there something you want to tell me?"

Chapter Two

Ethan was startled, and intrigued. With those few words, Elaine Montgomery had managed to turn his tactic around again. She was on a mission to stay in control, to manipulate him. Well, it wasn't going to work. This interview was not going to be easy, but it was definitely going to be interesting. He liked a challenge, and Laney Montgomery was definitely a challenge.

"Sure," he said. "I introduced myself earlier at the emergency room, but I think you might have been given something for pain. So in case you don't remember, I'm Detective Ethan—"

"I remember," she said flatly. "You were nicer then."

"Delancey," he went on as if she hadn't interrupted. "My partner, Dixon Lloyd, and I responded to the murder of Senator Darby Sills this morning."

"Detective Delancey, how long are you going to keep me here?"

He stood and stepped toward her, then propped his hip on the edge of the table, his thigh less than two inches away from her right hand. "It won't be too long. I just want to expand on our earlier discussion. Why don't you go through what happened from the moment you heard the noise from the sitting room? You told me that you walked in on the murderer within a couple of minutes of the sound of the first shot."

She scooted her chair away from him and

turned it toward him. "It was probably no more than twenty-five seconds," she corrected.

"Twenty-five seconds," Ethan said, jotting a note. "So what did the suspect do once he'd shot the senator?"

"During that twenty-five seconds? I don't know. I was opening the door and going into the sitting room."

Ethan sighed. He appreciated, but didn't like, her type of witness. She wouldn't let any fact slip by. Her account would be as accurate as she could make it. She wouldn't voice any assumptions either, unless he specifically asked her to. "Fine. What did he do when he or she saw you?"

"He, I think, judging by his build. He was thin, but that was about all I could tell in the dark. He turned toward me, lifted his gun hand and shot me."

Ethan knew the answers to a lot of these

questions, from the officers on the scene, from the crime scene unit and from the few seconds he'd talked with Laney earlier, but he wanted to hear her version. "Right or left hand?"

"Right hand."

"And what did you do?"

"I saw the gun and hit the floor," she said, touching the bandage gingerly. "Not quite fast enough, though."

"So you didn't actually see him pull the trigger."

"No, technically that's true." She lifted her gaze to his and lifted one brow. "But I would like to go on record as saying that I believe the same man who shot the senator shot me."

Ethan laughed at Laney's statement of the obvious. "Thanks for that insight, but that's not what I'm asking. My question is, did he fire the weapon with one hand or did he support his gun hand with his other?"

"I have absolutely no idea," she responded. "I wasn't looking at him when he shot me. Why would that even matter?"

"Mannerisms. Sometimes we can eliminate people based on how they handle a gun."

"When he first raised his hand, he just held the gun out, like this." She demonstrated. "Then I dived, he shot and I felt a burning pain here." She indicated the bandage.

Ethan waited a couple seconds, but she didn't continue. "What happened then?"

"My face was flat against the floor, my eyes were closed and my head was throbbing. At first, I was sure the shot had gone right through my skull. I expected a second bullet." She blinked and a small shudder vibrated through her shoulders. "But he didn't shoot again. I heard him walking toward me," she said, clasping her hands tightly together. "I heard one step, then two, then three. I knew he was coming to check me, to be sure I was dead. I remember praying, *Dear Lord, I don't want to die.*"

Ethan hadn't taken his gaze off her. Her eyes glistened with tears. Her fingertips and knuckles were white. She had believed that moment would be her last. He didn't speak. He waited for her to compose herself and get back to her description of what had happened.

With a small shrug, she said, "Then the elevator bell rang."

"The elevator?" Ethan echoed. She'd caught him off guard. He'd still been with her, in that awful endless moment when she'd feared dying. He'd been there, luckily only once or twice. But he'd known that helpless, hopeless fear. "What did the killer do?"

"He stopped and listened. I did, too. I was holding my breath. I mean, I didn't know who was on the elevator. It could have been somebody from the hotel staff or his accomplice. Who had access to the penthouse?" She suppressed a shudder. "Then I heard those shoes again."

"Those shoes?"

"What?" She seemed unaware of what she'd said. "Oh. Shoes. Right. His shoes sounded funny on the hardwood floor."

"Funny how?"

She gave him a puzzled look. "I'm not sure." Her voice held a tone of incredulity. Obviously, she wasn't used to being flummoxed.

"Come on, Elaine. You noticed them. Try to remember why."

Laney closed her eyes for a few seconds, then shook her head. "I don't know. They sounded—" she spread her hands out in front of her "—hollow? No. That's not quite right."

Ethan wrote down what she'd said, then looked up. "What does that mean? Hollow?"

"I don't know. I can't explain it."

"Okay. You were saying he headed the other way when the elevator bell rang. Which way?"

She closed her eyes again, then lifted a hand and pointed toward the left. "That way, toward the service door. When I opened my eyes my head started hurting and I must have moaned, because he turned back around and pointed his gun at me again. That's when the elevator doors started to open. He stood perfectly still for a second or two, like he was trying to decide whether to shoot me or run." She barked a soft, wry laugh. "He ran. Out the service door."

"He dropped the gun as he took off?"

She nodded. "Oh, and he was wobbly." She held her hands out and waggled them side-to-side. "The way he ran. Awkward, like he was about to fall down."

"Wobbly," Ethan repeated. "Had he tripped? Maybe hurt an ankle or twisted a knee?"

"No. I didn't notice anything like that. He just seemed unsteady on his feet."

Disappointed, he wrote down "wobbly and awkward." If the shooter had an injury, it might make him easier to find.

"The gun was found about halfway between the senator's body and the service door, and about seven feet away from you. Why did he drop it?" It was one of those things he couldn't figure out. Why leave the gun there? It didn't make sense. It telegraphed to anyone who cared to think about it that the piece would be untraceable. But there was no logical reason for the shooter to have abandoned it.

"I don't know."

"So who was on the elevator?" he asked her.

"A bellman carrying a bottle of Dewar's. Obviously, as soon as I left the room the senator called down and ordered it. I tried to tell the bellman that the killer was getting away, but my voice wouldn't work right. He saw me, though, and tried to help me." Her fingers went to the bandage. "I pointed toward the desk and told him to help the senator, but he was all freaked out by the blood, so I crawled over to the senator's body, and yelled at the bellman to call the police."

"You told him to call the police?" Ethan said. "Apparently he called hotel security instead."

"Did he?" she asked. "Oh. That's right. The security guard did show up first."

Ethan went back to his chair again. "Tell me more about the shooter. You said he was thin. What else? What did he look like? What did he have on?"

"He was about my height, thin and bony and dressed all in black. Had a black ski mask that covered his whole head. He was holding the gun—until he dropped it on the floor."

"Did you pick up the weapon or touch it in any way?"

"No," Laney said. "I know better than that. I've watched my share of *Law & Order*." Her hand went up to push her hair back, but her fingers skimmed the bandage and she grimaced.

Ethan scowled to himself. She was a little too sure of herself, a little too proud of what she knew. He'd love to tell her that about eighty percent of what she saw on *Law & Order* was as fictional as the names of the characters. But despite the fact that she got her forensic knowledge from a police procedural TV show, she was pretty smart. And despite the seriousness of the situation and his growing irritation at her attitude, he was fascinated by her. She had a confidence and a quick intelligence that he thought he'd like a lot under a different circumstance. For instance, if they were dating.

Forcing his attention back to the questioning,

he watched her as he said, "But you did move the body, didn't you?"

She started and brows shot up. "I did," she said. "I'd almost forgotten. I touched his shoulder and turned him onto his back. I shouldn't have done that, I guess."

While he let her think about that mistake, he consulted the statement of the first officer on the scene as well as his own notes. "Officer Young said you recognized something about the suspect?"

"I recognized something he was wearing," she corrected deliberately.

Ethan leaned back in his chair again. "What was that? I thought you said he was all in black."

"I did. But right before he ran, when he turned back toward me, something caught the light. It was a belt buckle. It looked like silver, but it was big. I only saw part of it. It looked like his shirt was covering more than half of it, but it reminded me of the belt that televangelist guy wears. The guy that always dresses in black. He's got that cowboy hat with the little silver things on it."

Ethan paged to the officer's report of his interview with her at the scene. She had told him essentially the same thing. He considered what she'd said and what was written in the statement. It was the closest she'd come to an outright lie. He'd bet next month's salary that she knew exactly who Buddy Davis was. "So are you saying the killer was wearing a Buddy Davis Silver Circle belt buckle?"

"Buddy Davis. That's him. Like I said, I didn't get but a glimpse of it, but that's what it looked like to me," she said, then narrowed her gaze. "But it couldn't have been Buddy Davis. He wouldn't kill anybody, would he?"

Behind the narrowed gaze, Ethan saw that

look again. That guarded caution. Combined with pretending that she didn't know who Buddy Davis was, it made him suspicious. Was she holding back something about the killer? Something about the belt buckle or about something else he'd been wearing? "I don't know. People are never predictable. The question is, do you think he would? Do you think it was Buddy Davis in that room?"

Laney looked down at the table. With one neat, unpainted fingernail, she traced a scratch in the scarred surface. "The guy was thin. But I can't really tell you anything else about him."

"Any other distinguishing marks? Did you recognize anything about the man?"

"If you mean about his appearance? No. I don't think so."

"What did you think when you first saw the buckle?"

"I guess my first thought was Buddy Davis,

but I didn't consciously think, *Oh, I wonder if that was Buddy Davis that just killed Senator Sills.*"

"Have you ever met Davis?"

She pressed her lips together again. "I have. Yes."

"Where?"

Her fingernail traced the scratch again and she spoke without looking up. "He and Senator Sills are—were friends. Everybody knows that. They golfed together about once every week or two."

Ethan was becoming more fascinated and more irritated with her every minute. Everything she said sounded perfectly reasonable, but it was obvious that she considered the consequences of every word she said first. He was more convinced than ever that she knew more than she was telling him. A lot more.

Now if he could only break through her confident demeanor and figure out what she was so carefully hiding from him. Would mentioning her father put a crack in that mask? "What about your father. Elliott Montgomery, right? He knew Senator Sills, didn't he? Isn't that how you got your job?"

Now she was the one caught off guard. And irritated at his implication. After a slight pause, she spoke. "My father. I wondered how long it would take before you brought him up. I assume you know he died last year. Heart attack."

Ethan remembered, now that she'd mentioned it. "I'm sorry."

"Thank you. But to answer your question, yes. He and Senator Sills had known each other for years."

"Were they friends?"

Her face shut down. If he had not been certain before that she was not telling him everything, he certainly was now. He waited for her answer.

"I don't think 'friends' is the word my father would use."

"What word would he use?"

Her gaze snapped to his. "What?"

He knew she'd heard him. He didn't answer.

"I don't know," she said finally. "Acquaintance? Business colleague?"

"Enemy?"

"No," she said quickly. "Why would you say that?"

He changed direction. "Did your father know Buddy Davis?"

"I'm sure they'd met, at least," she said. "I don't remember Davis ever coming to our house. And I don't remember ever seeing them together."

Nice. Clever, evasive answer. Ethan almost

smiled at her sheer audacity. "So is that a yes or a no?" he persisted.

She looked at him in silence for a moment and he could see the wheels turning in her brain. "It's a probably," she said.

She was good. He had to give her that. He had to admire her careful consideration of every question before answering. No assumptions. No guesses. What could he do with a probably? He had to act on it. He picked up his phone and pressed a button.

"Farrantino here," a brisk female voice said.

"Hey. Get Buddy Davis in here for questioning," he said. "ASAP."

There was a pause. "Buddy Davis?" Farrantino repeated. "The evangelist? That Buddy Davis?"

"That's the one. Problem?"

"No, sir." Farrantino's crisp tone was back. "I'll get right on it."

Ethan hung up. Laney had listened with unabashed interest.

"You're going to bring him in and question him just based on something I think I saw for about half a second?"

Ethan assessed her. "You think I shouldn't?"

"No. I mean, no, I don't think you shouldn't. I just—"

He waited.

She moistened her lips. "I don't know if I could swear that the logo was Davis's. I only saw a corner, maybe a little more. It did look like it, though."

He didn't comment. He just went on with his questioning. "So the killer, who had heard the elevator and wanted to get away, turned around enough that you could see a big gaudy belt buckle he was wearing?"

Laney shot him a suspicious glance, probably because of the tone of his voice. He hadn't meant to let his skepticism show, but maybe it wasn't a bad thing that she wondered if he believed her.

"Yes," she said shortly.

"Why?"

"He didn't say."

Ethan pressed his lips together, partly in irritation, partly to hide his smile. "Why do you think?"

"I think he was wondering if he had time to shoot me again."

"Hmm. Apparently he decided he didn't."

"Apparently."

"So what happened next?"

"Like I told you, he ran out the door and the bellman came in and called the police—well, hotel security—for me."

"Right," Ethan said. "And why was that?"

"Why was what?" she echoed, genuinely puzzled.

"Why him? Why didn't you call?" Ethan watched her. She was looking at her hands, and she seemed more at ease, now that they had left the subject of her father and Buddy Davis and were back to talking about what had happened.

"I was trying to get to the senator, to see if he was alive, so I yelled at the bellman to call."

"Didn't you have your phone with you?"

She shook her head. "No, I didn't," she said with exaggerated patience. "As I told the officer at the hotel, I'd left it on the computer table in the sitting room. I was trying to make myself get up and go back in there to get it when I heard the pop."

"The pop?" Ethan knew what she was talking about, but he wanted to hear her tell it. He'd read the hotel reports from the hotel's security guard and the first responding officer.

"You know, Detective, this might go a lot faster if you'd stop trying to trip me up. I've been over the pop I heard through the connecting door, too. I'm sure it's in the first responding officer's report." She gestured toward the folder open in front of him.

"I'm not trying to trip you up. And yes, the officer mentioned the sound you heard. But I'm asking you the question. I'm going to be asking you about a lot of things you've already told other people."

Her brows went up. "Yes, sir. Understood, sir," she said. "I heard the pop, so I got up to check on the senator. Then I—"

"Hang on. What did you think it was?"

"The pop?" She shook her head.

"You had an opinion about what you thought it was. Tell me."

"I'd rather not say," she replied. "It's not relevant."

"You let me decide what's relevant," Ethan said. "You just tell me."

She glared at him, but answered. "It was loud, but for a second I thought it might be a cork. Senator Sills enjoys a scotch now and then."

Ethan took mental note of the wry tone of her voice. "Did you hear anything else?"

She nodded, then winced. "A thud, as if something had fallen."

"And what did you think that was?"

"At the time I didn't know. But obviously it was when the senator fell."

"What time was that?"

"I'm not sure." She paused. "Don't the electronic locks on the rooms keep track of entries and exits by room number and time?" she asked.

Ethan smiled to himself. He liked the way she thought. Her attention to detail. His estimate of her level of intelligence kept going up. She was extremely smart. Irritatingly smart. Strangely enough, he liked that about her. "They can, but the hotel doesn't have that function turned on. The security guard said it would be cost-prohibitive to hire enough people to handle the amount of data all the comings and goings would dump into the computer."

"That's too bad. I can't imagine how the killer timed his attack on the senator so perfectly. I had just left the suite after making the last changes to the breakfast speech."

"I was wondering the same thing," Ethan replied evenly. He met her gaze.

She frowned. "You don't—oh, come on," she said, exasperated. "You don't think I'm involved in this? That's ridiculous. Senator Sills was my boss."

Ethan shrugged, watching her closely. Truth was, he didn't think she'd had anything to do with killing the senior senator. It was another attempt to catch her off guard. He wanted her rattled. Rattled and talking. "You surprised the killer, but he didn't kill you. He left you alive, knowing you might be able to identify him."

"He left me alive because someone was coming. But he knows I can't identify him. He was covered from head to toe in black. He *shot me*. Why would he do that if I were involved?"

"Maybe *he* wasn't there at all. Maybe you made him up."

"Oh, give me a break. You cannot be serious." She glared at him.

Ethan just watched her.

Her expression changed from irritation to surprise to frustration. She spread her hands. "Okay, then. I guess I'm getting the picture. So tell me, Detective. Am I under arrest? Should I have a lawyer? And don't bother telling me that if I was innocent I wouldn't need one. You might not think much of police shows on TV, but they do teach people a few things, like exercising their right to an attorney."

Finally, she was agitated. Her cautious demeanor was cracked. Ethan was glad. The confident, controlled person he'd seen in the hotel room and who'd walked into the interview room as if it belonged to her was gone, and in her place was a woman who had at the very least witnessed a murder and whose protective wall was cracking, piece by piece. And he knew—he *knew*—that he was getting closer to what she was hiding.

"I wouldn't dream of telling you that innocent people don't need lawyers. But you aren't under arrest. You are the victim of a crime and its only witness. You don't need a lawyer. I don't think you had anything to do with the senator's death. I do, however, think you're not telling me everything—"

"Why wouldn't I tell you everything?" she interrupted, spreading her hands. "I have nothing to hide."

"Really?" Ethan said, leaning back in his chair. "I think you do. I asked you before if your father's relationship with Sills was the reason Sills hired you. You didn't answer, but it's true, isn't it? The daughter of the infamous Elliott Montgomery, who lobbied for the Port of New Orleans Import/Export Council for over forty years, happens to be hired as Senator Darby Sills's personal assistant? How likely is that?"

A muscle ticked in her jaw for an instant, then she took a deep breath and let it out in a sigh. Then a little smirk quirked her lips. "Oh, come on, Detective *Delancey*. Nepotism has been a long and honored tradition in Louisiana. You of all people should know that. It has worked for generations without undue harm to anyone. Senator Sills was kind enough to let me intern with him for a year while I was getting my master's in political science." Her shoulders straightened. "He was pleased with my work, so he hired me. I don't see anything wrong with that."

Ethan gave her a hint of a smile. "Neither do I," he said.

She raised her brows. "Then what was all that?"

"Just demonstrating how you aren't telling me everything." He spent a few moments perusing his notes, not that he needed to. He wanted to keep her hanging for a little while, to demonstrate that he had the upper hand. Finally, he asked, "Is there anything else about the killer that you noticed?"

"No. I don't think so. The desk lamp was the only light, so the room was pretty dark. And of course he was in solid black."

"Not solid black," Ethan reminded her.

"No," she said, looking at him assessingly. "You're right. There was that belt buckle."

"Why do you think a killer who worked so hard to hide himself would put on something as distinctive as a Buddy Davis silver belt buckle?"

Laney shook her head. "I don't know, maybe to frame him."

Excellent guess. "But you're absolutely certain that's what you saw? You would swear under oath that it was one of Buddy Davis's solid silver belt buckles?"

"I told you, I'm not that certain. I thought the glimpse I got looked like one of them, but I can't swear to it."

"What *would* you swear to under oath?"

She shrugged. "I guess I'd say that I saw a large, oval silver belt buckle. I only saw it for a second and didn't see the whole thing because the man's shirt was covering it. I did see what looked like an engraved arc—possibly part of a circle, and an image inside the arc that looked like the edge of a crown. So if it wasn't Buddy Davis's Silver Circle belt buckle, it certainly bore a strong resemblance."

"That's about as precise a description as I've ever heard, even from experts," Ethan said, and meant it. She was an excellent witness. Irritating, but excellent.

"As Kate Hepburn said to Spencer Tracy in *Desk Set,* 'never assume.'"

"What? Desk set?"

Laney waved her hand. "Never mind. My dad loved the really old movies and the older TV shows, so I know way too much about them."

Ethan had never heard of the movie and he doubted seriously that it mattered, so he went on with his next question. "Describe what you did and what you saw when you crawled over to check on the senator."

"I was hoping he'd done what I had—dived to the floor, hidden under the desk, something.

But—" She shook her head and a shadow crossed her face. "He was dead."

"Did you touch him?"

She nodded, pressing her lips together. Ethan noticed that her eyes shone with tears. "Yes. I turned him over to see where he'd been shot. But as I said before, his eyes were…dead."

"Then what did you do?"

"I listened to see if I could hear him breathing, and I felt his neck, trying to find his carotid pulse. By that time the security guard was there. Almost no time later, the police officers showed up, and then you." She spread her hands as if to show him that she had nothing else.

Ethan watched her thoughtfully, letting the silence stretch, as he had earlier. He waited to see if she'd break the silence this time, because, while he had no idea if the information she was guarding so closely had anything to do with the murder of Senator Sills, he knew with a hundred-percent certainty that she was still holding back.

After a few moments, she looked at her watch. "It's after noon. I need to call the senator's family. I have to tell them—"

"That's been taken care of," he said with a wave of his hand. She'd broken the spell of silence without revealing anything—again. She was good. He'd like to have her on his team in a fight.

"What is your precise position on Senator Sills's staff?"

She fixed him with a frosty glare. "My *precise position* is personal assistant to Senator Sills."

Ethan nodded and jotted "personal assistant" on his pad. "And what are your duties as the senator's personal assistant?"

If possible, the glare turned even colder. Had he sounded sarcastic?

"Pretty much what you'd expect. I wake him up every morning, make sure his meals are to his liking and on time. I type up his personal correspondence, update his social media pages, keep up with his appointment calendar and his committee schedules, and—"

"So you're his secretary."

Her shoulders stiffened. "No. He has a secretary. She works in Baton Rouge. I travel—traveled with him wherever he went."

"Okay. You're more of an administrator."

"I suppose you could say that. I do a lot of administrative work. I also edit the memos and letters the secretary sends over for his signature, and often, I stamp them with his signature stamp. Especially all the congressional letters we send out in response to constituent problems."

"You also travel with him and stay with him?"

Ethan hadn't figured her shoulders could get any more stiff, but she managed it. "Many of my duties are last-minute. So yes, I generally will stay in an adjoining room near him in case he needs something in the middle of the night."

"What kind of things did Senator Sills need in the middle of the night?"

Now she was becoming visibly angry. "Last night he worked on his speech until after eleven o'clock," she said through gritted teeth. "So I didn't finish typing the last revision until after midnight. Then—"

The door to the interview room opened and Ethan's partner stepped inside, smiling in a friendly manner. "Afternoon, Ms. Montgomery. I'm Detective Dixon Lloyd."

Elaine Montgomery gave Dixon a smile like nothing he'd seen from her yet. "Nice to meet you. Please call me Laney. You must be Good

Cop, because Detective Delancey here is definitely Bad Cop."

"You have no idea," Dixon said.

At the same time, Ethan asked loudly, "What's up, Dixon?"

Dixon handed him a file folder. "We got the report back on the weapon that killed Senator Sills. There's a partial print on the barrel. Probably not enough for a positive ID. It could be marginally helpful along with other evidence."

"Did they check it against Ms. Montgomery's prints?"

Dixon nodded. "First thing. No match."

"I didn't touch the gun," she said.

"And therefore your prints were not found on it," Ethan said evenly.

"You want me to stay and play good cop?" Dixon asked, obviously noticing the tension between them.

"No," Ethan said firmly.

At the same time, Laney said, "Yes."

"Okay, I'm going," Dixon said on a laugh, reaching for the doorknob. "Oh," he said, reaching into his pocket and coming out with a piece of paper. "Here's a note I was told to give to you." He handed it to Ethan.

Ethan skimmed it. "Is he serious?" The note was from Commander Wharton. He wanted an in-person report from Ethan about the Whitley and Stamps interviews. "He should have the transcriptions on his desk by now."

Dixon shrugged. "I'm just the messenger."

"Did he ask you to come, too?"

Dixon shook his head.

"That figures. I suspect his real question will be if I've interviewed Travis." Ethan sighed. "Wait for me outside, will you, Dix?" Ethan said.

He turned to Laney. "Despite my partner's amusement, this is a very serious matter, Ms.

Montgomery," Ethan said. "I realize that you are a victim, just like Senator Sills, but you're also the only witness to his murder. I don't have to tell you how much publicity is going to be surrounding this case, especially in light of Congressman Whitley's involvement in the kidnapping of Max Chalmet."

"Oh, you certainly don't have to tell me anything about that, Detective *Delancey*. I read the paper. I'm perfectly aware of the latest scandal involving the Delanceys."

Ethan bristled. "The *scandal* didn't involve the Delanceys. The scandal was the kidnapping plan cooked up by Gavin Whitley, who by the way did his best to implicate your boss."

"Congressman Whitley was mistaken. Senator Sills had nothing to do with that."

"And you would know because—?"

"I know because I'm—" She paused. "I was his personal assistant."

"The fact that you worked for him isn't proof that he wasn't involved in the kidnapping. You say you know. How?"

"I handled all his correspondence. All of his phone calls go through me."

"All?" Ethan laughed. "Can you prove that?"

"I—" She stopped and Ethan knew she'd gotten to the place where he'd been ever since she'd said *I know because*— Of course she couldn't prove it.

Ethan pushed back his chair and got up.

"Oh, good. Are we done now?" Laney asked, sliding her chair backward. "Because I have a lot to do. There is a checklist a mile long that includes who all is to be notified, who is to be invited to the wake and to the funeral, *where* the wake and funeral are to be, how the family should be brought in—"

Ethan held up a hand to stop her. "I get the

picture. Are you the only one who manages all that?"

"No. I believe the office of the governor and the office of the president of the senate handle most of it, but they'll be calling me—in fact, I'll need my phone."

"Nope. You're not going anywhere or making or receiving phone calls until I'm finished with you, and right now I've got to go see my commanding officer. So while I'm gone, I need you to write out your duties as Senator Sills's personal assistant, and write an accounting of your and the senator's time from the moment you got to the hotel."

Laney's shoulders stiffened. "Then I'll ask you again. Am I under arrest?"

"No," he said, "but I would rather you didn't leave."

She looked at him, irritation evident in those eyes again, but she didn't speak.

"If I think of anything else I'll have one of the officers let you know," Ethan said as he opened the door and left the room.

Chapter Three

"What do you need, Delancey?" Dixon asked after Ethan closed the door to the interview room. "I'm late. I've got officers on the way to Sills's home to confiscate all his personal records. We're still waiting to hear from the court order filed with the bank."

"Did you check the Chalmet kidnapping case file to see if they already requested his bank records?'

"Yep. We got his checking and savings accounts and CD records. What we're waiting on is access to the safe-deposit box."

"Good," Ethan said.

"So has she mentioned anything about Sills having trouble with anyone or receiving threats from anyone?"

"Not yet, but then, I only started questioning her." Ethan rubbed his eyes. "But I've got to tell you, I'm not happy about the names that have already popped up."

"What names?"

"You know who she is?"

"Yeah. Elaine—Montgomery."

Ethan nodded grimly.

"Wait a minute. Montgomery—" Dixon frowned. "Her father wasn't the lobbyist—?"

"Yep. Elliott Montgomery."

"So the lobbyist's daughter is working for a prominent state senator who's been known to be influenced by the large interests represented by the Port of New Orleans lobbyists and unions," Dixon said.

"And who just got murdered. Yeah. But that's not the biggest shocker," Ethan replied.

"It isn't? What else have you got?"

"Did you talk to her at the crime scene? Or anywhere?"

"No. I left her to you. I've been dealing with the mundane, day-to-day stuff."

"Yeah, well, it serves you right. You're married. You *shouldn't* be talking to pretty young witnesses."

"What about the big shocker?"

"Right. Get this. According to her, the man who shot Sills was wearing a great big silver belt buckle. She saw it when it reflected the light. Want to guess what she saw on it?"

"No." Dixon grimaced.

"A crown and circle."

Dixon stared at him. "Please tell me you're kidding me."

"Not even a little bit. She claims a patch of

bright silver caught the light. She only caught a glimpse of it but she's sure she saw a part of a circle and the corner of a crown."

Dixon pushed his fingers through his hair. "Is she willing to testify to that?"

Ethan shook his head. "I don't know. She's sure of what she saw, but she only saw part of the buckle. The rest was obscured, apparently by the shirt. A really good defense attorney could probably make her look at worst like a liar and at best, like that graze on her temple is causing hallucinations."

"What do you think? Think she really saw that belt? Delancey, do you think Buddy Davis shot Senator Sills?"

"I don't know," Ethan said. "But I know what I've got to do. I've sent Farrantino to pick up Buddy Davis and bring him in for questioning. I'm not looking forward to that. Talk about a media circus."

Dixon smirked. "You sent Farrantino? I'd love to be a fly on the wall when she confronts Davis. Everybody in the state knows his reputation for *paying attention to* pretty women."

Officer Maria Farrantino was tall and lithe, with long black hair. Even with her hair pulled back and dressed in the androgynous police uniform, she was a knockout. "I figured he might come in just to get to ride in the car with her," Ethan said. "But do not tell her I said that."

"Did you warn her to watch out?"

"Didn't get a chance," Ethan said.

"Like hell you didn't. Oh, she's never going to forgive you. It should be interesting with Davis and his wife together in the car. I don't think I'll stick around for the fireworks—Benita Davis's or Farrantino's." Dixon checked his watch. "I've got to get going," Dixon said.

"Yeah, and I've got to go tell the commander

what he's already read on the transcribed interviews," Ethan said on a frustrated sigh. "Let me know if you find anything interesting in Sills's house, like records of blackmail or proof that he bought or sold votes in the legislature."

Dixon laughed. "Right. You'll be the first to know."

LANEY MONTGOMERY DIVIDED her attention between the door through which Detective Ethan Delancey had just disappeared and the mirror on the wall in front of her. She wondered how many people were standing on the other side of that mirror, watching her. Then she wondered just how paranoid she was to think that. Still, she figured there was one person in there at least—the handsome, arrogant detective.

She wondered if the "note" Good Cop had given him was real, or just an excuse to let him get out of the room for a few minutes.

She had a childish urge to stick her tongue out—maybe even stick her thumbs in her ears and waggle her fingers. But Detective Delancey apparently already thought she was hilarious. She hadn't missed him suppressing a smile every so often as he listened to her answers to his questions. There was no need to make him think she was also immature.

She wondered why he, a Delancey, had become a police detective. Like everyone else in Louisiana, she'd heard of Con Delancey, the infamous politician who was beloved by his constituents. The word was that although the Delancey patriarch had provided generous trust funds for each of his grandchildren, they all worked—several as police officers, either in New Orleans or in Chef Voleur on the north shore of Lake Pontchartrain, Con Delancey's hometown. She'd also heard that the Delancey men were charming as well as handsome. She was forced to agree with the handsome part, but she was still waiting to see the charming side of Detective Ethan Delancey.

She glanced at the two-way mirror again. Almost as powerful as the urge to stick her tongue out was the urge to turn her back on the mirror, or better yet, just get up and walk out of the room and the police station, leaving Ethan Delancey to like it or lump it.

But she didn't have the nerve to do either. His tone when he'd told her he'd *rather* she didn't leave had sounded like an order. If that were the only consideration, she might risk it. After all, he'd admitted she wasn't under arrest. But to her dismay and chagrin, she realized she didn't want to let him down. For some reason, she didn't want to see disappointment in his blue eyes. She liked it better when they sparkled with humor or danced with what she would like to think was interest. *Interest?* She didn't mean interest. She meant amusement. She wanted to make him laugh. He seemed much too serious. His face didn't have the natural creases that laughter pressed into the skin around eyes, cheeks and mouth. His mouth was wide and straight, and he had a strong jaw and his eyes were killer sexy. She'd love to see them crinkled in laughter. The most she'd managed to coax out of him was a slightly crooked smile so small it might be better labeled a smirk.

She rubbed the back of her neck and closed her aching eyes. She felt grimy and exhausted. She hadn't slept a wink and it was—she peeked at her watch—after two in the afternoon. Almost twelve hours since she'd surprised the murderer in Senator Sills's suite.

She considered banging on the mirror and asking for a quiet place to lie down and take a nap. Or maybe she could sleep in here. She scanned the walls for a light switch, but didn't see even one. Did that mean the lights were controlled from outside the room? She'd watched the television versions of police tormenting suspects to obtain information, even confessions. Were some of those stories true?

She was beginning to see why suspects confessed, even if they were innocent, at least on TV shows. She was about ready to declare that she had shot the senator because he made one too many changes to his speech, if it meant they'd let her go home and take a shower. She was exhausted, and her head was pounding. She wanted privacy. *Craved* it. She wanted to be at home, in bed with the covers pulled over her head. And she wanted to stay there until this nightmare was over.

But she'd never been able to just stick her head in the sand—not even as a little girl. She'd been born with the talent—or curse—of an almost uncanny intuition. Her mother had died when she was eleven, but she'd known, years before, that her mother was sick. She'd also figured out that her mother's illness was not the kind that was talked about in public. Then, later, she'd realized that her dad's late nights and mysterious meetings with people like Senator Sills were also best kept as secrets. Even though she didn't know exactly what went on, she always knew that there was something wrong about them.

Her first thought after she'd recovered from the shock of seeing the senator dead was that her life, from that moment on, would never be the same. Her brain had gone into fast-forward, detailing the consequences of any action on her part a week, a month, a year in the future, like a desert highway that stretched on to the horizon and beyond.

She would be tied up with inquiries, hearings, trials for who knew how long. Her career was toast, and privacy was something she might never have again. She was smack in the middle of the biggest murder case to hit New Orleans since Con Delancey's personal assistant had killed him twenty-five years ago.

Then a more immediate concern hit her. The killer had seen her. Did he realize she couldn't identify him? Did he care? The idea that the person who had killed Senator Sills in cold blood was out there, maybe waiting for a chance to kill her was terrifying. For an adrenaline-soaked second, her limbs tightened in an almost uncontrollable urge to run.

But where? She was in the police station, probably the safest place in the area, at least for now.

Once she'd calmed down and settled into the hard-backed chair again, she thought about the senator and reflected on how selfish she was being. Quelling the urge to touch the bandage above her temple, she reminded herself harshly that she was alive. The senator was dead. Her dad was dead. But each of them in their way had left her a legacy—a heavy, burdensome legacy that she would have to unload before she could ever be free of the past.

Exerting an almost superhuman effort to keep her face expressionless in case there were people on the other side of the mirror watching her, Laney pulled the legal pad the detective had left on the desk toward her and began to write down her duties as personal assistant to Senator Darby Sills.

By the time she finished documenting everything the senator had done since he'd arrived at the hotel the afternoon before, Detective Delancey was back.

As he closed the door, she asked, "How much longer are you going to keep me here?"

"Why? Have you got some place you need to be?" Ethan snapped, frowning.

She lifted her chin at his tone. "Actually I do. I'm going to be receiving a lot of phone calls—condolences, questions, comments. I'd like to have my phone so I can check my messages periodically, if you don't mind."

He nodded toward the legal pad. "Did you finish giving me a written accounting of your duties and Senator Sills's and your movements yesterday?"

"Yes. It's all here. Can I get my phone and purse so I can go?"

Ethan turned toward the mirror. "Have Ms. Montgomery's belongings brought down here," he said.

While they waited, he leaned back in his chair and watched her. Those blue eyes on her made her extremely uncomfortable. But she did her best not to show it. She pulled the legal pad to her and read over what she'd written— or pretended to.

Even without looking at him, Laney felt Ethan Delancey's presence. She'd noticed last night in the penthouse suite that the feel of the whole room changed the moment he walked in. From the first instant she'd laid eyes on him, she noticed an energy about him that seemed almost palpable. She remembered glancing around to assess others' reactions to him, but most of the other people in the room were going about their tasks as if nothing was different. Was it just her?

And now, as tired as she was, as sick of this room and the police and the questions as she was, she still felt that same energy. But there was something else, too. Something calming or soothing. All her tension and exhaustion didn't fade away, but it occurred to her that she'd felt very alone and uneasy while he'd been gone. Now that he was back, she felt safe.

She glanced up to catch him watching her. Her heart rate shot up and she quickly dropped her gaze back to the pad. On second thought— maybe that feeling of safety was just wishful thinking—or a hallucination.

He said something she didn't catch. She looked up. "What?"

His mouth quirked into a ghost of a smile. "I asked if you're ready to go. Were you falling asleep?"

"No," she snapped, then blinked as she realized he had her purse and her phone. Her gaze went to the door, which was closed, then back to him. Had she dozed off for a few seconds? Long enough for someone to bring her things in without her even noticing?

"Hey," she blurted as she realized he was

playing with her phone. "What are you doing? That's my phone."

At that instant, another phone rang. "Don't worry. I'm just using it to call my phone. There," he said as the phone stopped ringing. "Now you've got my phone number. And I've got yours."

She looked at him, puzzled. "Why?" she asked.

"Just in case," he said. "If you think of anything else that might be pertinent to the case, or if you need anything, you can just call me." He pushed her phone across the table to her.

With a shrug, she slid it into her purse. "Okay, thanks." She stood and sidled past him toward the door.

"Laney," he said, his voice close to her ear.

A shiver slid through her as she turned her head.

"Stick close to home. Don't go out alone,

especially at night. The killer knows who you are."

The shiver became a frisson of fear gripping her spine. "But he knows that I have no idea who he is, right? I mean, I couldn't see anything except that mask."

"And the belt buckle," Ethan reminded her. "And Laney, we're holding on to that clue. Don't tell anyone about it. Not the press, not anyone in the government. Not *anyone.*"

"You think someone in the legislature might be involved?"

"I don't know. Right now, I'm proceeding as if everybody's involved until I can eliminate them."

She shrugged, reached for the doorknob, then turned back. "But I'm not a suspect, right? You still know I didn't have anything to do with the senator's murder, don't you?"

"I can't totally rule you out as a suspect yet,

but no. Personally, I don't think you're involved," he said. "However—"

"However what?" she asked. To her dismay, her voice quivered slightly.

"You could be in danger," he said.

Although she already knew she could be targeted by the man who'd killed Senator Sills, his words ramped up the chill of fear inside her. "In danger. From the murderer?"

"He knows who you are. I'm going to have one of the police cruisers in the area drive by your house every few hours, just to be safe."

He reached around her and opened the door. She caught the clean scent of soap and shampoo. "I'll walk you out."

As they walked down the hall from the interview room, two well-dressed men were standing near the front entrance to the station, straightening their ties and talking in undertones to each other. Laney recognized one of them, Senator Myron Stamps.

Beside her, Ethan muttered a curse. He laid his hand reassuringly on the small of her back.

Reassuring, yes. His warm hand felt like a promise of safety, but she couldn't help but be suspicious at the timing. Had he set up this *accidental* meeting to see how she would react when confronted by one of the two members of what Senator Sills had called the "Good Ole Boys" club? It had been long rumored that Sills, Stamps and Whitley, a trio of older politicians in the Louisiana Legislature, had taken bribes and kickbacks from businessmen and lobbyists in the import/export businesses to keep taxes low and look the other way when certain illegal substances were brought in through the Port of New Orleans. In fact, the kidnapping of Dr. Kate Chalmet's little boy had been a warped plan to keep Stamps in office so the graft and corruption could continue.

As if he could hear Laney's thoughts, Senator Stamps turned. Unsure what to do or say, meeting him in the middle of the police station, Laney pasted on a small smile and nodded.

Senator Stamps stepped forward. "Laney," he said, reaching out a hand toward her, but Ethan stepped in front of her. "Excuse us, Senator," he said evenly.

"I just wanted to speak to Laney," Stamps countered, and spoke to Laney as if Ethan wasn't there. "My dear, you must be in shock and terrified." Stamps squinted at the bandage on her head. "Oh, my dear, were you shot?"

Laney opened her mouth, but Ethan deflected the senator again. "I'm sorry, Senator. It's probably best if y'all don't communicate."

Stamps frowned as Ethan guided her past him. Beyond, Laney saw the other man, probably Stamps's lawyer, scowl. Was his disapproval aimed at Stamps, at Ethan—or at her? She nodded to him as well, but he just glared at her.

Laney held her tongue until Ethan had opened the door to the squad room and guided her through and out the front door of the station house.

"Why did you do that?" she demanded, once they were walking down the concrete steps.

"Do I have to remind you that you are a victim in this case, as well as my only witness, and Senator Stamps is a person of interest. You shouldn't be talking to him."

"Not that. Why did you walk me right past them?"

Ethan frowned. "That was an accident."

"You mean you weren't hoping for an encounter? You weren't hoping someone would say something incriminating?"

"It didn't hurt my feelings that Stamps confronted you."

"He wasn't confronting me. He was offering his condolences."

"His lawyer should have stopped him. Didn't you see the look he sent him?"

"I can't say if it was aimed at Stamps or you or me."

Ethan said, "Listen to me. You need to be careful. Don't take any unnecessary chances. Don't go out alone at night."

"So you do think I'm in danger. But not from Senator Stamps, surely?" she asked. "I thought you figured any threats would come from Buddy Davis. Assuming he was the man in black."

Ethan glanced around as they stepped off the bottom step and onto the sidewalk. "Watch what you say in public. And as for threats or danger, until I have some concrete evidence,

I'm considering everybody dangerous, especially to you."

Laney frowned at him. Suddenly, his voice had gone harsh.

"You've got my number. If anything, and I mean anything, odd or unusual happens, you call me. Got it?"

She angled her head for a second. "Yes, sir," she said, still not sure how she felt about his seeming certainty that something could happen to her. "I will call you at the first sign of a roach, a scorpion or a thug with a gun." She smiled.

But Ethan didn't. He scowled at her. "This is not a game, Laney." He reached out and touched the bandage on her temple. "I'm not trying to scare you. I'm trying to make sure you stay safe. The killer shot at you because he wanted you dead. If his aim had been a quarter-inch lower, you would be."

Chapter Four

By the time Laney got home, it was after five in the afternoon, fifteen hours since Senator Sills had been killed. She flopped down on the sofa, too tired to even kick off her shoes. Her eyes filled with tears, mostly from reaction to the long, awful night and day. The sight of the senator dead on the floor and the feel of the bullet grazing her temple seemed at once glaringly real and a terrifying nightmare.

She hadn't minded working for the senator, but she hadn't particularly cared for him as a person. Of course she was sad that he was dead. Sad for him and for his two daughters. They would be devastated. One of them had a new baby. The senator had been so excited and so proud. She'd never met them, but she wondered if she ought to call them.

What would she say? She couldn't tell them anything about the murder, couldn't tell them anything she'd seen or heard. She couldn't tell them about the man in black. Ethan Delancey had warned her not to talk about the case and he'd told her that the police had taken care of notifying the senator's family. It was likely that the only thing she would accomplish would be to upset them.

The senator's daughters were not the only people she didn't know how to handle. She had dozens of messages on her phone from people who had called while she'd been stuck in that interview room at the police station. And by the time she'd gotten into her car and headed home, her phone was ringing almost constantly. She had no idea what to say to any of them either.

She'd turned the ringer off and done her best to ignore the vibration whenever it rang. Now as she sat on the couch in her living room and tried to relax, she heard it vibrating in her purse, which sat on the table in the foyer. With a sigh, she pushed herself to her feet and retrieved it. Back on the couch, she started playing messages and returning calls. There were several from Senator Sills's other staff members, wanting to know what had happened, was she okay, had she seen anything. She tried to keep her conversation with each of them short and her answers generic and vague, but every single staff member, from his secretary to his campaign manager, begged her to tell *just* him or her and swore they would not tell a soul.

While she talked to them the calls kept coming in. She screened several more and was surprised and irritated to hear other legislators' staffers, whom she knew as speaking acquaintances, asking the same questions that Sills's staffers had ask—was she all right, had she seen anything, if she'd tell them what happened they wouldn't tell a soul. She deleted their messages. The last message was from her best friend, who'd sounded so frantic that Laney immediately called her back and did her best to assure her that she was fine.

By the time she'd listened to probably forty calls and returned more than twenty of them, her head was hurting and she was so tired that she could barely move. But staying on the couch in the clothes she'd worn for the past thirty hours or more was not an option.

With a great deal of effort, she pushed herself up off the couch and forced herself to walk to the kitchen and open the refrigerator. The contents included a carton of milk that was probably out of date, a take-out box of Chinese food from—she counted backward—four days ago, a carton of eggs, a package of shredded cheddar cheese and two cans of decaffeinated cola. She considered a cheese omelet, but even that sounded too difficult. Sighing, she closed the door and drew herself a glass of water from the dispenser on the front.

Before she could even take a swallow her phone rang again. She looked at the display. It was a number she didn't know. Probably another congressman's staffer, fishing for information.

As she went into her bedroom, she turned the phone off. She put it and her glass of water on the nightstand and looked at her bed. She wanted to collapse into it and fall straight to sleep. But there was one thing she wanted more than sleep. A shower. She headed to the bathroom, discarding clothes along the way.

Within seconds, she was under the hot shower spray. Again, the tears welled in her eyes. Weariness, sadness, fear. She could take her pick of emotions. Standing there with the warm water loosening her tense muscles as it washed away the dirt and grime, she knew what she was really crying about. She'd been there. Right there in the room, a few scant feet from the man who had murdered Senator Sills in cold blood, and she hadn't been able to do a thing about it. She couldn't even identify him.

In that moment, staring up at him from the floor, she'd felt more helpless than she ever had in her life. Helpless and terrified and crushingly guilty.

She'd never been Senator Sills's biggest fan, mostly on behalf of her father, but she had never wished him dead. But he was dead, and for the life of her, she couldn't figure out what she could have done to save him. Her brain began inventing scenarios—what if she'd not gone to her room when she did? What if she'd jumped up immediately when she heard the pop?

Ethan's voice came back to her from the E.R., when he was being nice. *You couldn't have done anything. Not against a gun. If you'd tried, you'd probably be dead now, too.* The words weren't very comforting, but somehow, they helped. Or maybe it wasn't the words. Maybe it was him. The timbre of his voice. During that brief time, unlike the interrogation at the police precinct, he'd spoken gently, even kindly. When his eyes turned smoky and soft, she would believe anything he said.

She closed her eyes and let the hot water cascade over her, washing her fear and guilt down the drain, at least for a while. The image of

Ethan Delancey's hard-planed face and smoky eyes helped her relax. As she washed, she realized that her hands were lingering on certain areas of her body and her languid relaxation was morphing into a pleasurable tension. Not the sharp, electric tension of fear and guilt. No. This was different. It swirled, building slowly, spiraling from the deepest center of her desire out to her suddenly sensitized skin. She lifted her head and let the shower spray caress and tease her breasts. As she drew a deep, moisture-laden breath, the water began to cool.

She shivered and wrenched off the water taps. Quickly, she ran a towel over her body, which suddenly felt too heavy to lift. Wrapping a terry cloth robe around her and using the damp towel to squeeze the last droplets of water out of her hair, she headed into her bedroom and threw back the covers.

Then she dropped the robe and slid into bed.

She snuggled under the covers with a relieved sigh. Closing her eyes, she searched her brain for the image of Ethan's smoky eyes, but that spell was broken. As she'd turned off the hot, seductive shower and dried her body, she'd also turned off the hot, seductive daydreams.

It was as though stepping back into the cool real world had erased all that. Now all she could picture was Ethan's mouth as it twisted into an annoying smirk at things she'd said, or inverted into a frown when he didn't like her answer. It was obvious that he could turn the kindness on and off at will. And clearly, his default attitude was officious and annoying. She wondered how that worked for him when he wanted information from witnesses or suspects.

Her last thought before she fell asleep was that she needed to get her dad's financial records before it occurred to Detective Ethan Delancey to get a warrant for them.

SHE WOKE TO the sound of gunfire. A muffled pop that had her cringing, paralyzed with fear, until she fought her way to consciousness and realized she'd been dreaming. She opened her eyes to darkness and lay there, listening. Two more pops sounded, and then—a car's engine revved and tires squealed.

Laney collapsed back into the bedclothes, her limbs quivering with relief. The pops were nothing. Just a car's engine backfiring. She wasn't in the hotel room facing a killer. She was home in her own house. She was safe.

Safe. The word immediately conjured Ethan's words. *I'm not trying to scare you. I'm trying to make sure you stay safe.* With those words and the memory of his smoky eyes reassuring her, she relaxed and drifted toward slumber. But her fickle brain began to wonder what time it was. Sighing, she glanced over at her silent phone, then with a groan, reached out and picked it up.

Turning it on, she saw the time. Eleven-thirty. She'd been asleep for about four hours. Then with a cringe of dread, she looked at her phone log. There was a long list of numbers she didn't recognize. But she saw a missed call from her Aunt Darla, in Philadelphia. That meant that Senator Sills's murder had made the national news.

She pressed redial and spoke to her father's sister for a few minutes, assuring her that she was all right and declining to come to Philadelphia to visit. She explained to her aunt that she had to stay here during the investigation into the senator's killing. She didn't mention to her that she'd been a witness or a victim.

When she ended the call, she turned the

phone off again, feeling much less guilty and somewhat self-righteous that she'd interrupted her much-needed sleep to check her messages. As soon as she closed her eyes, she fell asleep and dreamed that it was Ethan who got off the elevator and rescued her from the murderer.

THE NEXT TIME she woke, it was to a loud banging that set her heart to racing. She reached for her phone to see what time it was, but it was turned off. So she threw back the covers to get up—and discovered that she was naked.

For a second she just stared at herself in disbelief. She had never gone to bed completely naked before—and with wet hair, too. She must have been exhausted. The last thing she remembered was the exquisite sensations the hot water sluicing over her skin caused.

The banging forgotten, she closed her eyes,

but it started again and a loud familiar voice cried, "Laney! Laney Montgomery! It's Ethan."

Ethan. Detective Delancey. What was he doing here? She jerked the sheet up to cover her breasts, then sniffed in embarrassed amusement. She was alone in the room. *For now.*

She pushed the covers back and got out of bed, wondering what she could throw on that would sufficiently cover her nakedness. And what the hell was Ethan Delancey doing outside her door at—whatever time it was in the morning anyhow?

She scurried into the bathroom, trying to suppress the urge to cover herself with her hands as if he could see through the walls. She splashed water on her face and glanced in the mirror. She'd gone to sleep with wet hair and this morning it looked like Medusa's snakes. She ran her wet hands through it, trying to smooth it. Then she looked at the robes and gowns on the back of the door. No. She wanted her terry cloth robe. It was white and thick and covered her from chin to toes. Likely the most modest piece of clothing she owned, as long as the sash at the waist stayed closed and the front flaps didn't slip.

But where was it? She glanced through the bathroom door at her bed. There it was, right where she'd left it last night. She tiptoed over to the bed and quickly threw it on. She wrapped the robe tightly around her and cinched the sash as tightly as she could. Then she hurried down the hall to the front door.

Just as she reached to unlock the deadbolt, Ethan banged again. "Laney? Are you in there? I swear if you don't answer the door I'm going to break it down. Are you okay in there?"

She took a deep breath. "I'm—I'm here," she said. "Just a minute."

"Laney? It's Ethan."

"I know," she cried. "Hold on." She finally got the door open.

Ethan was standing there, on her front stoop, his pressed white shirt unbuttoned over a white T-shirt and his hair uncombed. "Thank goodness," he said when he saw her. "I was afraid something had happened to you. Do you know that your phone is off?"

She nodded.

"Well, turn it on. Don't you know people are trying to call you? I called several times. I figured you might have turned your phone off while you were asleep, but it's eight-thirty."

"Eight-thirty? Oh, my God. I slept for over twelve hours."

"Well, that's good, I guess," he said. "Aren't you going to invite me in?"

Laney glanced behind her. "I—uh, well I just got up and—" She instinctively stepped out of the way as he walked inside, closing the door behind him. He surveyed the foyer and the rooms that opened onto it—the living room to his right, the kitchen directly in front of him and a hallway to his left. There were three doors on the hall—bedrooms and a bathroom he figured.

Laney watched him take in her little house. His expression didn't change, but his head moved slightly in what she thought might be a nod.

"Got coffee?"

"I can…make some," she said with a vague gesture toward the kitchen. But then she stopped. She had no reason to extend hospitality to him. He'd shown up at her door banging and making a scene. She turned to face him. "What are you doing here?" she asked.

She started to put her hands on her hips, but felt the terry cloth sash give a little and decided a better idea would be to fold her arms across her middle, anchoring the robe in place.

He headed into the kitchen. "The coffee's not made," he said, looking at the pot and then at her.

"No, it's not," she said. "I asked you a question."

"I'm here because I need you to come in to sign your statement. Can you be there at ten?"

Laney looked at her kitchen clock. "That's barely over an hour from now."

"Yeah," he said, opening the cabinet above her coffeepot, spotting a can of coffee and retrieving it. "Plenty of time."

He inspected her pot, emptied the reusable filter, rinsed it and refilled it with fresh coffee. He filled the carafe with water and poured it into the pot, then turned on the power.

"No," she said. "It's not plenty of time. Oh,

and please, make yourself at home," she added sarcastically.

He glanced at her, first in puzzlement, then understanding. "I figured I'd better make the coffee if I wanted some, since you're busy holding your robe together," he commented, a small smile curving his lips. It wasn't wry but it wasn't kind either. It was more…suggestive.

His gaze drifted downward to the neckline of the robe. It took all her willpower not to look down. But she couldn't stop her face from heating up. She knew she was blushing.

"What's the matter?" he asked, studying her face. "You said you got over twelve hours of sleep. You obviously showered, by the look of your hair."

She shot her fingers through her damp hair, smoothing it as well as she could.

"Is that—" he inclined his head toward her hair "—going to keep you from getting dressed and down to the station by ten?" He didn't take his eyes off her, just stood there, waiting for her to answer.

"No," she said through gritted teeth. "Of course I can be there by ten, if that's what I have to do."

"Great," he said. "I'd appreciate it." He turned back to the coffeepot, watching it drip. After a couple of moments, he looked back at her. "Shouldn't you be getting ready?"

"Shouldn't I—" Laney drew a deep breath. Although the vestiges of the dream in which Ethan heroically saved her from the black-clad monster in the hotel room still lingered, she couldn't remember for the life of her what had made her think that it would be romantic to be rescued by him. He was arrogant, impatient and rude. In fact, she was sure if he had the occasion to rescue her, she'd never hear the end of it. She cleared her throat. "I thought I'd have a cup of coffee first," she said coldly.

"Okay," he said. "Good idea. Where are your mugs?"

"Here," she said, pulling one from the cabinet and edging past him to pour it full of coffee. She turned and handed the steaming mug to him. "Please," she said with a smile. "Keep it. Drink the coffee on your way to work."

He looked at her in mild surprise, gave her that same little smile he'd shown her earlier, lifted the cup in a coffee salute, then turned on his heel and left her house, stopping to salute her one more time at the front door.

Laney poured herself a mug of coffee, although what she wanted to do was slide back down under the warm covers and go to sleep again. She knew, however, that by the time she did something with her hair, dressed and drove to the police station, she'd be lucky if it wasn't after ten.

She headed to her bedroom to put on underwear and clothes, but first, before she took off the terry cloth robe, she looked at herself in the full-length mirror on the back of the bathroom door. Had Ethan known that she had no clothes on under her robe? She'd thought the thick cotton was the best thing to cover her, but now, trying to see what he'd seen, she realized with embarrassment that a fluffy white bath robe and wet hair said nothing so much as *I'm just out of the shower and didn't bother to dress.*

BUDDY DAVIS, FOUNDER and pastor of the Silver Circle Church on the North Shore of Lake Pontchartrain and owner of the Silver Circle Broadcasting Network and Circle of Faith Ministries, sat in the interview room with his wife and business partner, Benita. The two of them had their heads together and Benita seemed to be doing most of the talking.

Ethan watched them through the two-way mirror in the viewing room. Maria Farrantino stood at his side.

"You sent me out there to get them on purpose, didn't you?" she asked.

"What? Me?" Ethan said innocently. "Nah. I'd have gone yesterday, but they were up in Jackson. Thanks, by the way, for bringing them in."

"He practically groped me, right there in front of his wife. And she acted like I was coming on to *him*."

"He does have that reputation. Remember when that female deacon in his ministry accused him of sexual harassment?"

"*You'll* be accused of sexual harassment if you do anything like that again."

"I apologize for his actions, Farrantino, but

you know you're going to have to take them home, too. I'll call you when they're done."

"Oh, no. No. No. No. Their chauffeur followed us. He's waiting for them in their limo. They do not need a ride home."

"They'll need to be escorted from the building," he said teasingly.

"Don't push it, Delancey."

"Seriously, I didn't mean to put you in that situation," he said. "I'm planning to walk them out."

"I can do it," she retorted. "Don't think I can't handle him."

Ethan shook his head. "No. I want to do it. I'm working on a theory."

"Hey, fine. Do what you want. I'd be happy if I never saw that skinny Richard Petty wannabe again." She left the room.

Ethan turned his full attention back to Davis. He did look like a pale copy of the legendary NASCAR race driver in his black cowboy shirt, tie, leather jacket and jeans, and sporting a graying mustache. Against all the black, the signature silver belt buckle he wore stood out like a beacon. Small replicas of the buckle circled the black cowboy hat that completed his outfit. As they'd walked through the station, Buddy had shaken hands with and spoken to every single person he passed. And the whole time, Benita, his wife of thirty-some years, had clung to his side, her arm through his, and smiled and greeted people right alongside him.

Davis's wife was an interesting specimen. She was several inches shorter than Davis and the description that came to Ethan's mind was lean and hungry. Even though she had to be in her late fifties or early sixties, she wore a sleeveless top and a short denim skirt with cowboy boots. She obviously spent a lot of time either outside or in a tanning bed. He was reminded of an obsessed runner whose primary goal in life was zero body fat. She was leaning near Davis's ear with her hand on his shoulder and talking rapidly.

Ethan was not looking forward to this interview. He'd questioned his share of celebrities, local and national, and he knew that he was going to encounter outrage, defensiveness, entitlement, pompousness, irrational demands and probably a quick dismissal with those words every police officer dreads hearing. *I want my lawyer.*

He sighed as he walked around from the viewing room to the interview room. He'd give it his best shot until they cut him off. He'd no sooner stepped through the door when Benita attacked him verbally.

"What's your name? I'm going to report you. How dare you send a rookie bimbo to bring us in here, without even a courtesy call ahead of time? This is an outrage. I've got a good mind to demand to see your captain."

"Benni," Buddy Davis said gently, placing a hand over hers. "Why don't we listen and see what the young man has to say." He turned his mild blue eyes to Ethan. "Are you a detective, son?" he asked, smiling.

"Yes, sir," Ethan said. "Detective Ethan Delancey." He chose to respond to the evangelist rather than to his strident, outraged wife. He'd heard bits and pieces of Davis's sermons on television. The man was as hellfire-and-brimstone as any TV preacher Ethan had ever heard. But he'd never met Davis. The contrast between Buddy Davis the evangelist who dressed outrageously and drove a fancy Italian sports car while he shouted and ranted about love and tolerance, and Buddy Davis the polite,

kindly husband who calmed his wife and sub-
tly offered amends to Ethan, was astonishing.

"Delancey," Buddy said, smiling. "I never
met your granddad, although I'd have liked to.
He was a powerful and influential man. I was
sad when he died."

"Thank you, sir," Ethan said as Benita continued her tirade.

"And another thing," she said stridently.
"Why have we been dragged in here against
our will? What on earth—"

"Against your will?" Ethan interrupted.
"Surely the officer didn't force you? Please
tell me she didn't handcuff you or hold you at
gunpoint."

Benita flushed. "Of course not. If—if she
had, I would have already called our lawyer.
But she practically threatened us."

"Practically," Ethan repeated thoughtfully. "I

see." He greeted Davis, smiling at him. "Mr. Davis—" he started.

"*Pastor* Davis," Benita cut in.

"I beg your pardon," he said. "Pastor Davis, I'm sure you've seen the news about Senator Sills."

"Of course he has," Benita said. "It's all over TV, radio and the internet."

Davis patted her hand again. "Benni, he's just doing his job. Let me answer his questions and we can be on our way."

"Ma'am," Ethan said, turning his attention to her. "If I have to, I'll separate you. I need to be able to question Pastor Davis without you interrupting."

Her face twisted in anger, but before she could speak, Davis's hand squeezed hers. With a grimace, she tossed her head as if to say, *Go ahead, but you're going to regret it.*

"Thank you. Now, Pastor Davis," Ethan said. "I take it you've seen the news?"

"Yes," Davis responded. "It's awful. Someone murdering Darby Sills right there in his hotel room."

"Did you know the senator?"

"Why, yes. We are—or we were—good friends. We've played golf together for years."

Ethan nodded. "That's right. Senator Sills's personal assistant, Elaine Montgomery, told me that." He threw the name out, then paused, waiting for a reaction. Buddy Davis didn't react, but Benita appeared to be almost in apoplexy from biting her tongue. "You know who she is, right?"

"Who? Elaine?" Davis asked. "Oh, yes, of course. Pretty thing, isn't she? She must take after her mother, because she's certainly better-looking than her old dad." Davis laughed.

"Her dad. That would be Elliott Montgomery. You knew him?"

"Excuse me, *Detective.* I don't mean to butt in, but why are you asking *us* about Senator Sills's murder?"

"We're talking with everyone who knew the senator, starting with those he had spoken with recently."

"That certainly does not include us."

Ethan addressed his answer to Buddy. "There was a call from the senator's cell phone to your phone yesterday."

"What?" Benita snapped. "Buddy? Did you talk to Senator Sills?"

Buddy looked at her. "I—I'm not sure," he said.

"Where's your phone, Buddy?" she asked him.

"Right here, in my pocket."

"Let me see it."

Buddy pulled his phone out and handed it to Benita. She bent her head and studied it, punching a button here and there.

Ethan divided his attention between Buddy and Benita. Their relationship seemed odd. As hellfire-and-brimstone as Buddy was when he preached, he was as meek as a lamb sitting here talking to his wife. Benita, for her part, was loud and insistent on his behalf but soft-spoken, even cautious, when talking to him. What was up with these two?

"Here it is," Benita said. "The call came from Senator Sills's cell phone but it's showing as a missed call. I knew Buddy hadn't talked to him. Here, Buddy. Take your phone." She handed it to him, then turned back to Ethan. "Will there be anything else, Detective?"

"As a matter of fact, yes. I have a few more questions. Pastor?" he addressed Buddy. "I was asking about Elliott Montgomery. Did you know him?"

"Montgomery?" Buddy repeated.

"The lobbyist, honey," Benita said, patting Buddy's hand. She turned to Ethan. "We met him a few times at political functions or charity events," Benita answered. "I don't recall ever meeting his daughter, though." She shot a glance that was at once possessive and filled with suspicion at her husband.

"I just know her from going to Darby's office, Benni. And I saw her a few times when she was younger, with her dad." He paused. "Did something happen to her, Detective? I certainly hope she wasn't there—"

"Buddy!" Benita snapped.

Ethan shot her a look. What was that about? Was she trying to shut him up before he said something incriminating? "No, sir. Nothing has happened to her. You were saying?"

Buddy frowned at him. "I was saying?"

"You said you certainly hoped that Elaine Montgomery wasn't there."

Buddy's frown deepened and he looked at Benita.

"Don't worry about it." She laid a hand on his arm. "He was just expressing his hope that Ms. Montgomery was all right. Now, is that all?"

"Pastor," Ethan said, ignoring Benita. "Where were you at around two a.m. on Wednesday morning?"

Buddy squinted at him. "Two a.m.? When? Yesterday?"

"Yes, sir," Ethan said. "About thirty or so hours ago."

"Well son, at two a.m. I'm pretty sure I was at home asleep." He looked at his wife. "Right, Benni?"

Ethan noticed that as strident and interruptive as Benita had been throughout the questioning so far, she was uncharacteristically tight-lipped now. "Ms. Davis?"

She looked up. "What? Oh, sweetie, of course you were." She inclined her head toward Buddy while nodding at Ethan. "Snoring like a freight train. We haven't slept in the same room in years. I can't sleep a wink if we're in the same room, with all that honking and blowing going on. But he's always in bed by eleven." She swallowed. "Always."

Buddy nodded placidly.

"And what about you, Mrs. Davis?"

"Me? You mean where was I when the senator was killed? What a ridiculous question. Are you suggesting that I might be a suspect?"

"My job is to ask questions, ma'am. Could you please answer?"

"Ask Buddy. I was at home in bed asleep, too."

"But the two of you were in separate rooms.

So really, neither one of you can swear that the other was at home."

"Hmm, Benni? I think the boy's got a point there," Buddy said with an appreciative smile.

"Don't be ridiculous," Benita snapped at the same time. "We were there, in the same house, all night."

Ethan let the silence stretch for a moment, to see if either of them would break it. Benita was back to biting her lip and Buddy just stared at a spot on the desk. After about forty seconds, Ethan spoke. "So exactly what time did you last see your husband that night?"

"Well, it had to be close to eleven, didn't it, since as I just told you, he goes to bed by eleven."

"*Had to be?* You don't remember for certain?"

She glared at him. "What I don't remember is the past few nights being any different than our usual routine."

Nice, Ethan thought. Benita Davis was quick and careful.

"What about you, Pastor Davis? What time do you remember last seeing your wife that night?"

"What night was that again?" Buddy asked, looking at his wife.

Ethan started to answer, but Benita broke in. "I think that's enough." She stood, making a production out of checking her watch. "We have to be somewhere. Are we under arrest, Detective?"

"No, ma'am," Ethan said. "I just have a couple more questions."

"Let's go, Buddy. We're leaving."

Buddy frowned at her. "Benni, we shouldn't be rude. That's not the Christian way. You know what I always say. *Be kind, live life and—*" he stopped, glancing down at his hands.

"Love your neighbor," Benita said with a

smile that looked stiff to Ethan. "That's exactly what you say, and what a wonderful rule for living life. Don't you agree, Detective?"

That was odd. Ethan studied Buddy for a moment, watching him perk up and continue talking about the Christian way to live one's life. When Buddy was done, he gave Ethan a small smile and sat back in his chair, looking satisfied and smug.

On the other hand, Benita was a mini-volcano ready to explode. Her frustration and anger had been building ever since she walked into the station. It seemed that Buddy's short soliloquy only added heat to her fire. Ethan was absolutely sure that she was going to blow her top within about twenty seconds. He studied her. When she finally blew, would she accidentally spill something she didn't intend to? He could hope, he supposed.

There was nothing Ethan would like more

than to burst Benita's angry balloon, and he knew exactly what would do it—whether or not the evangelist or his wife were guilty.

He stood. "I want to thank you for coming in," he said, smiling at them both. "I hope that if anything else comes up, I can speak to you again."

"I'm not sure why you would need to talk to us again. We have nothing to do with Senator Sills or anything that happened to him."

"In any case, I need to warn you not to leave town. We may need to question you again."

"You may—?" Benita repeated. "You *may* need to question us again? This is unconscionable. Well, I *may* need to speak to Leon."

Leon was, of course, New Orleans Police Department Superintendent Leon Fortenberry. Ethan smiled at her, hoping the right amount of wistfulness showed. "I think that would be a really good idea. I receive my orders from

Superintendent Fortenberry's office. So I'd actually welcome you speaking directly to him. He can discuss with you how vital your cooperation is to our investigation."

"Fine. We're going there right now." She held out her hand to Buddy, and he took it and stood.

Ethan nodded reluctantly. "That's your prerogative, Mrs. Davis." He turned to Buddy. "Thank you, Pastor." He paused, looking at Buddy's waist. "You know, that belt buckle of yours," he said. "I couldn't help but notice it when you came in. It's pretty distinctive."

Buddy beamed. "Why thank you, son. I'm really proud of that. Did you know Benni designed the logo? Silver Circle. It stands for our Silver Circle of Faith."

"Silver Circle of Faith. What is that?" Ethan asked.

"Wait a minute. What's got you so all-fired interested in the silver belt buckle anyhow?"

Benita asked sharply. "What's it got to do with anything?"

Ethan feigned surprise as he turned to her. "Why, nothing. I was just admiring it. Have I upset you in some way?"

Benita glared at him. "You haven't upset me. I just want to know what that belt buckle's got to do with Sills's murder."

Ethan spread his hands. "I wasn't suggesting it had anything to do with it. Please forgive me if I gave you the wrong impression. I was just curious."

"Oh, please," Benita huffed. "You brought us here to question us about Senator Sills's murder. Now, suddenly you're talking about belt buckles. You'd better do a better job than that of explaining yourself."

"There's nothing to explain," Ethan went on, mildly. "I merely made a comment. Do *you* have any reason to think the buckle has something to do with the senator's murder?"

An odd expression passed across Benita's face. A flash of confusion or paranoia. It faded immediately, but Ethan knew he'd seen it.

Buddy said, "What in the world could my Silver Circle belt buckle have to do with the senator's death?" Buddy asked. "I thought he was shot."

"Nothing," Benita said firmly, patting Buddy's hand. "Absolutely nothing." Her earlier confusion was gone. "Detective Delancey has no idea what he's talking about. There are only around twenty-five in existence. They're worth around five thousand dollars each. And fourteen of them are in our safe at the house."

"Fourteen out of twenty-five. Well, that makes them pretty rare, doesn't it?" Ethan asked with a smile. "When was the last time you checked on those you have in your safe? Are you sure you know how many are in there?"

"Oh, good grief," Benita exclaimed, disgusted.

Buddy answered. "I doubt the safe's been opened since the latest Silver Circle Award was bestowed upon a deserving member of our congregation." He frowned at Ethan. "Son, you never answered my question either. Why are you asking about the belt buckles? Does this have something to do with Darby?"

Ethan took a deep breath and prepared to make the Davises suspicious of his motives. "I really can't say," he said. He waved toward the door of the interview room. "Come with me. I'll walk you out."

As he stepped over and opened the door, holding it for Buddy and Benita, he could feel Benita's searing gaze burning the nape of his neck. Good. Now they'd be worried.

He glanced at his watch. Ten-thirty. Laney should be out front, waiting for him. Probably had been for the past half hour. He'd told the desk sergeant to seat her directly on the aisle from the front door to the interview room. He wanted Laney and the Davises to meet face-to-face, and he wanted to be there to observe all three of them. "Well, I want to emphasize how much I appreciate you coming down here to talk with me," he said as the three of them stepped into the hall.

"You don't fool me, *Detective*," Benita assured him. "You're trying to get a rise out of us by talking about the belt buckles. Well, it won't work. You'll be hearing from Leon about your disrespectful behavior. And you'll hear from our lawyer, as soon as I talk with him about what charges we're going to bring against you."

"Mrs. Davis, I hope your meeting with the

superintendent will be more satisfying that this one has been for you."

"Don't you worry," Benita growled. She narrowed her gaze at him for a few seconds, started to say something else, then caught herself. "It will," she said.

Ethan nodded solemnly. "Please don't forget. You need to stay in town, in case we do have more questions for you." He led them through the halls to the front desk. "Thank you again. If you'll excuse me, the desk sergeant has something for me."

He started toward the desk then stopped. "Oh, and by the way, can you call and let me know for sure how many of those belt buckles are in your safe? It will save us both some time and trouble if I don't have to get a warrant."

Benita turned red but Buddy took her hand and she clamped her mouth shut.

Ethan smiled as he walked over to the front

desk. On the way, he nodded at Laney, gesturing to her that he'd be with her in one minute. Then he leaned on the high counter and started a conversation with the sergeant.

Buddy and Benita walked between the desks toward the front doors. Ethan turned to watch as the two of them came face-to-face with Laney. When she looked up and saw Buddy, her brow furrowed and she sent a quick, accusatory glance toward Ethan. Buddy saw her and smiled admiringly, as he did with every pretty young woman he saw, but as far as Ethan could tell, there was nothing else. Buddy either didn't recognize her or he was one of the best, slickest criminals Ethan had ever seen. And judging by the contrast between his sermons and his behavior today, he just might be that slick.

Then Laney turned her gaze toward Benita and her eyes widened.

From Ethan's vantage point, he could see Benita clearly. The woman aimed a scathing glance at Laney, then turned to her husband. "Come on, Buddy," she said, sliding her arm into his. "Let's get out of here. Next time we see you, Detective, or *any* of your officers, we will have our attorneys present."

Ethan tipped an imaginary hat at her. "I wouldn't have it any other way, ma'am."

Chapter Five

"That was Buddy Davis, wasn't it?" Laney asked Ethan as he guided her into the interview room where she'd waited for so many hours the day before.

"Yes, it was," he said.

"And was that woman his wife? Benita Davis? I've heard she's the real power behind Silver Circle of Faith Ministries."

"She's a piece of work. I can tell you that. What did you think when you saw them?" he asked her.

"Nothing really. I mean, Buddy's build—I

suppose he could have been the man in black, but her—what's her name?"

"Benita."

"Right. Benita. She looked as though she knew me and hated my guts."

"Hmm," he said.

"What do you mean, hmm?"

"She could have been jealous because I mentioned your name to them and Buddy remembered meeting you."

"Oh, great. So she does hate me," Laney said. "Thanks."

"You want some coffee? A cold drink?" Ethan asked, choosing to ignore her sarcasm.

She sent him a wry smile. "So now you're playing good cop. Will the other detective, the tall handsome one, be playing bad cop today?"

"Handsome?" Ethan echoed.

He looked slightly taken aback. She smiled to herself. Was he not used to his partner getting the attention from females? Granted, the taller, dark-haired detective had on a wedding band; and did a couple of inches really matter between two guys who were both six feet tall? She'd wanted to goad Ethan Delancey a bit, and she'd succeeded.

"I apologize. Did I hurt your feelings?"

Ethan smiled reluctantly. "No. It's just that I have never once thought of that ugly mug as handsome in any sense of the word."

"Well, you're not a girl."

"No, I'm not. I'm glad you realize that."

"Are you?" Laney didn't know what the difference was today, but Ethan, sitting across the table from her in his white shirt and dress pants, seemed to have gotten over whatever his problem had been with her the day before. In fact, if she weren't mistaken, she could believe that he was actually flirting with her. Not seriously, of course. He was still the cop and she was still the victim, the witness and possibly one of the suspects.

She gave her shoulders a mental shrug. She was probably totally wrong. He probably wasn't flirting at all. He could have had a headache yesterday, or a hangover. Maybe he got some sleep last night, too, and just felt generally friendlier today.

She glanced up and caught his gaze. He looked thoughtful and faintly puzzled. "What?" she asked.

"Wondering what you meant just now. Am I what? A girl or glad?" he asked. "Girl, no. Glad…yes." His smile widened.

She almost gulped. He *was* flirting. The question now was, was he doing it consciously or unconsciously? She decided her best bet was to ignore it. "So is my statement ready to be signed?" she asked.

"Your statement." He blinked, then stood.

"I'll be right back." He left, shutting the door behind him.

Laney frowned. That was odd. He'd told her to be at the station at ten to sign the statement, then he'd kept her waiting for over half an hour while he talked to Buddy Davis and his wife. Now he'd demanded she come down here, he'd put her in the interview room, but forgotten about the statement. Strange.

She glanced at the two-way mirror. Was there something else at play here? Was he standing back there on the other side of that mirror and watching her? Waiting for her to do—what? There was nothing in the room except a short number two pencil lying on the table. She sent the mirror a mischievous look and picked up the pencil. What if she defaced the already-defaced table by carving her initials into it? Was that considered destroying city property? Maybe she could write some nasty graffiti on the walls, although the paint was such a musty gray already that her excellent penciled poetry might not even be visible. What if she stabbed herself with the pencil point? Would they put her under suicide watch and make her talk with a psychiatrist? Would they think she was a stronger candidate for killing the senator?

With a small laugh she tossed the pencil down. Maybe Detective Delancey was just absentminded this morning and really had forgotten to get the statement.

The door opened and he came in, hanging up his phone and pocketing it as he did so. "Sorry. We're going to have to do this later. I've been called to the superintendent's office. I have to go immediately."

Laney frowned, seeing his empty hands. "If you have it, I could read it over and sign it while I'm here. You don't have to be here, do you?"

He shook his head. "For some reason the transcriptionist couldn't lay her hands on it. I'll give you a call. Sorry for your trouble." He stood there beside the open door, waiting for her to get up and leave.

"No problem," she said, standing and walking out past him.

Ethan fell into step beside her. "I'll see you out. I'm headed out to my car anyhow."

"Where's yours?" he asked as they walked down the steps to the sidewalk.

She pointed to a fifteen-minute parking place down the street from the police station.

"Okay. Mine's over here in the police lot. We'll get that statement signed maybe tomorrow."

"Not tomorrow. I have to drive up to Baton Rouge for a meeting about Senator Sills's funeral and who's going to finish out his term."

"Okay. Well, we'll get together. When's his funeral—and where?" Ethan asked as he turned toward the police parking lot.

"We're finalizing that today, with his daughters. I'm guessing it will be Sunday morning in Baton Rouge. From what I've heard, his younger daughter will be taking him to Shreveport to be buried. That's where his parents are."

"Any idea who they'll choose to finish out his term?"

Laney shook her head. "Not a clue," she said. "He's divorced, so it won't be his wife. I'm sure I'll know more after this meeting tomorrow."

"Yeah," Ethan muttered noncommittally. "Okay. I'll see you—"

His words were cut off by a town car speeding past, too close to the curb. Laney backed up instinctively and Ethan grabbed her, pulling her back against him as she turned to look at the license plate.

"*'Silver Circle 1,'*" he said as she focused on the vanity tag.

"Oh, my God," she whispered breathlessly.

"Are you all right?" he asked, still holding her close. His strong yet gentle fingers were wrapped around her upper arms and her back was pressed tightly against him. She felt his fast, steady breaths and the lean hard planes of his chest and abs.

"I'm okay." Her voice was shaky and she knew the tremor was only partly because of the close call. Some of it was her sudden, unwanted awareness of Detective Ethan Delancey's fine, hard body. *No, it's not fine,* she corrected herself, consciously pulling away from him.

He let her go, after a brief hesitation.

"Was that really—?" she started.

"Buddy and Benita," Ethan grated. "Benita's probably still pissed at me for hauling them in for questioning. I ought to have them picked up for reckless driving."

"But who was driving? It wasn't either of them, was it?"

"Can you describe the driver?"

She closed her eyes, thinking. "He was larger—muscle I think, rather than fat. He had black hair, kind of curly or wavy. That's all I can remember."

"Good job. I didn't notice the hair being wavy or curly." He was staring in the direction that the car disappeared.

"Do you think they were really trying to hit us?"

"No, he just got as close to the curb as he could, and he sped up as he came closer. They may not have been seriously trying to hit us," Ethan said grimly, "but it was definitely a threat."

EVEN THOUGH IT was only around noon when Laney got back to her house, she felt as if she'd been up another twenty-four hours. The sleep she'd gotten the day before suddenly seemed too far in the past to remember. She had nothing to do tonight except screen and return phone calls, so she'd stopped at the grocery store and bought mascarpone cheese, Parmesan cheese, angel hair pasta and a box of frozen spinach. After setting her purse on the foyer table, she put the grocery bags on the kitchen counter and dug in it for the spinach. She tossed the unopened package into the microwave and set it for defrost.

Ten-minute spinach Alfredo was her go-to dinner, and today, because she thought she deserved it, she'd bought a bottle of wine. All that was required for the sauce was butter, mascarpone cheese, garlic, spinach and plenty of Parmesan cheese. Within about seven or eight minutes, just the right time to cook angel hair pasta, the meal was ready. Paired with a good dry white wine it was manna from heaven. And if she had enough left over to last the rest of the week, so much the better.

While she waited for the spinach to defrost, she checked her phone. Twelve messages. She ran through them quickly. More acquaintances wanting to know what she knew, a call from a TV station asking for an interview and Senator Sills's secretary reminding her of the meetings tomorrow. By the time she'd reviewed and deleted them all, her eyelids were drooping. She had a long, quiet afternoon stretching ahead of her, perfect for a nap before dinner.

She put the cheese and the defrosted spinach into the refrigerator, then headed down the hall to her bedroom. She'd sleep for a couple of hours, then get up and make the pasta. She was looking forward to curling up on her couch and eating while she watched the news. Then back to bed, and maybe, by the next morning, she'd feel as if she'd finally caught up on her sleep.

THE NEXT THING Laney knew, someone was knocking on her door. Before she came fully awake, she dreamed it was Ethan, coming to check on her again. So when she opened her eyes and realized it was dark outside, she was surprised and, at first, a little disoriented.

It took her a few seconds to remember that it wasn't morning. She'd lain down for a nap after getting home from the police station. But how long had she slept? The knock sounded again, startling her. *Oh, right.* Someone was at the door.

She swung her legs over the side of the bed and slipped on her shoes. She hadn't undressed to nap, so she still had on the shirt and slacks she'd worn this morning. She went into the foyer and called out, "Who is it?"

A soft female voice said, "Hello? Hi in there. My name is Carolyn. I live a few houses down. I think my cat may be under your car."

Laney sighed in frustration. Carolyn sounded young and perky and newly married, and Laney did not want to deal with her. *Sorry. Can't help you if you don't have sense enough to keep your cat inside,* she wanted to say. Instead she settled for a dismissive "Your what?" hoping that *Carolyn* would go away. She didn't want to be pulled into the woman's cat drama.

"Uh—my cat. Please? She's a kitten. Can you help me?"

With an explosive sigh, Laney opened the door a crack and peered through it. A young woman in rather tight blue pants and a striped sweater stood there, smiling warily and holding a cheap flashlight. "Oh, hi. I'm Carolyn." She held out a hand but Laney wasn't in the mood. She hung on to the door.

Undeterred, Carolyn continued. "Okay, then. Hi. We just moved in and my cat got out when I came home a little while ago. I've been looking for her and I think she's under your car. Do you think you could help me?"

"Have you tried calling it?" Laney asked, not yet convinced that her help was needed to get the silly feline out from under her car.

"Well, yes, I have," Carolyn said archly.

Whoa. Maybe that was unnecessarily rude. "Okay," she said reluctantly. "I'm not sure what I can do—"

"Do you have a flashlight?" Carolyn asked, pointing hers at Laney and turning it on. A feeble glow was all that the bulb could manage. "Mine's dying."

"Just a minute," Laney said and turned on her heel, as Carolyn stepped into the foyer. She had a very good flashlight somewhere. She looked in three kitchen drawers before she found it.

When she got back to the door, Carolyn was tapping the head of her flashlight against her palm and then looking straight at it. "Now it's completely dead," she said woefully. She looked at Laney. "Oh, that's a nice flashlight."

"Mmm-hmm," Laney responded as she gestured to Carolyn to lead the way to the lurking cat. Carolyn walked around the side of the house to Laney's car and crossed to the far side. "I think she's closer to this side. Can you bring the flashlight over here?"

Laney rolled her eyes. Yes, she was acting bitchy, but she'd had a difficult couple of days. Much more difficult than losing a cat. *Lost your cat? Well, I was shot by the man who'd just murdered my boss.* Taking a deep breath, she told herself that she should just get into the spirit of finding the cat, because the sooner the cat and Carolyn were back safe at home, the sooner Laney could get to her pasta and wine.

"Okay," she said, a little more energetically as she walked around the car and crouched down. "What color is the kitty?"

"She's white with a little black spot right here." Carolyn pointed to the middle of her forehead. "So cute and only about three months old." Carolyn knelt gingerly, as if she were afraid her pants would split.

Laney sank to hands and knees, doing her best not to scuff her shoes, and peered under the car. "I don't see anything."

"I'm afraid she could be up under the hood," Carolyn wailed.

"Maybe I should start the engine," Laney said drily, knowing that if the cat were in the engine compartment, cranking the car could be the end of kitty.

"Do you think that would work?" Carolyn asked, wide-eyed.

"No."

"Oh."

Laney thought she saw a hint of anger cross Carolyn's plump face. The expression twisted her bland, wide-eyed countenance into a face that seemed oddly familiar. But it was dark out, and Laney was still in that drowsy waking-up-from-a-deep-sleep haze, so she wasn't completely sure.

Then Carolyn brightened. "I know," she said excitedly. "I'll go on the other side and you stay on this side and shine the flashlight under the car. I'll call her. Maybe the light plus the sound of my voice will make her come to me."

"Maybe," Laney muttered. "Are you sure the cat didn't run while you were at my door?"

"I don't think so," Carolyn said as she walked back around the car. "Bend down again and shine the light," she said.

Laney did as she was told, doing her best not to wish evil plagues on Carolyn and her cat.

"Oh, look!" Carolyn cried.

Laney stood. "What?"

"It's Binkie!" She pointed behind Laney. "She's running back toward our house." Carolyn squealed and clapped her hands delightedly.

Laney looked at her askance, then turned, but saw nothing resembling a white cat. "You saw her?"

Carolyn nodded eagerly. "I'll bet she'll be waiting at the door when I get there," she said, scurrying up the street.

"Do you want to borrow my flashlight?" Laney called after her.

"No. We're fine."

Laney shrugged and headed inside, closing and locking the door. She opened the refrigerator to take out the makings for spinach pasta. But just as she'd stacked the container of cheese on top of the spinach and was reaching for the butter, the doorbell rang again.

"Oh, no you don't," she whispered. "I am not going after that cat again." She walked to the foyer and called out, "Who is it?"

"Uh—hi. It's Carolyn again. I forgot something."

"What?" Laney snapped.

"Your phone."

"My—" Laney wasn't sure she'd heard right. "My phone? What are you talking about?"

"I found it on the ground," Carolyn said. "I meant to hand it to you but I forgot."

Laney glanced down at her purse. "I wasn't carrying my phone. It must be somebody else's."

"It was right beside your car—on the driver's side."

"That's imposs—" She stopped herself. Maybe when she climbed out of the car? "Hang on a minute." She felt around inside her purse, but she didn't feel the familiar cool rectangular shape of her smartphone. She emptied her purse onto the foyer table. No. Her phone wasn't there. Baffled, she felt the pockets of her slacks. Not there either.

Shaking her head, she stood and unlocked the door. "What color is it?"

Carolyn stood there, holding a phone in a white case. "Here you go," she said with a smile. "This is yours, isn't it?"

Laney took the phone. "It's mine," she said, puzzled. She felt as if she'd just been pranked.

"Thanks again for helping me," Carolyn said, waggling her fingers. "Bye." She whirled and sashayed down the steps.

After closing the door and locking it with a determined twist, Laney stood there in the foyer, looking at her phone. It had a few specks of dirt on it. *Lying beside the car on the driver's side.* It must have dropped out of her purse, although she wasn't sure how it could have.

Oh, well. It was lucky that Carolyn found it. Otherwise it would have lain outside all night, and there was a prediction of heavy showers.

ETHAN WAS ON his way to Laney's house when his phone rang. He'd decided to take her statement to her and get it signed tonight, telling himself that if she were gone all day tomorrow, it would be another day before her official signed statement got into the file, and that was just sloppy paperwork. Plus, it wouldn't hurt to check on her, make sure she was doing okay.

What he wasn't doing was making up an excuse to see her. Okay, maybe he was, but it was for her benefit. He just wanted to be sure she was safe at home, after that incident with Buddy Davis's car on the sidewalk that afternoon.

The phone rang again.

"Delancey. Where y'at?" Dixon said when Ethan answered. It was a common casual greeting in New Orleans, but usually when Dixon said it, he meant it literally.

"In my car, headed—home." He didn't want his partner to know he was checking on Laney. He wasn't sure why.

"Good. Got any brandy?"

"Sure. That bottle of Courvoisier you brought over around Christmas is still there. Why? You have a fight with my cousin?"

"No. Rose's mom is at the house with her. They're shopping online for baby clothes."

Ethan smiled and rubbed a place in the middle of his chest where he felt a twinge. "How's she doing?" His partner had married his cousin Rosemary, whom he'd tracked down after she'd been missing and presumed dead for over a decade. Dixon had been ridiculously happy ever since, but now that they were expecting their first child, he was over the moon.

Ethan had felt an odd twinge under his breastbone ever since Dixon had told him about the baby. He rubbed the place in the center of his chest again.

"She's fine. Feeling great," Dixon said, sounding impatient.

So Dixon was not inviting himself over to talk about babies or the joys of marriage this evening. That was fine with Ethan. He'd had enough of Dixon's parental joy to last him a long time.

He figured that Dixon must want to talk about something related to the search warrant he'd executed at Senator Sills's home in Baton Rouge. It had taken Dixon and three forensics specialists two days to confiscate all of the personal papers in Sills's house, box and transport them back to New Orleans, and organize them in an empty conference room at the courthouse. "So what's up then?" he asked. "Did you unearth something at Sills's house?"

"How far are you from your apartment?"

"About three minutes," Ethan replied, taking the next left and heading back toward Prytania Street.

"Okay. See you in ten. Pour me a double brandy."

"You got it."

Ethan had changed into jeans and had the brandy poured by the time Dixon arrived. "Come on in and take a load off," he said when Dixon knocked on the screen door after clomping up the wooden staircase to Ethan's second-story walk-up.

"Thanks," Dixon said, picking up the snifter of brandy that sat on the table Ethan used as a bar. He sat in the recliner next to the couch where Ethan was stretched out.

"Have you eaten? Want to order pizza or something?" Ethan asked.

"Nah. Rose has something for me when I get home."

"Chips?" Ethan nodded toward a crumpled bag of potato chips on the coffee table.

"I'm good." Dixon took a sip of brandy. He sighed and settled more deeply into the recliner.

"So what's up?" Ethan set his soft drink down and dug into the chips.

"We executed the warrant on Sills's residence yesterday."

"Yeah, I heard. A lot of paperwork. I guess he was planning on writing his memoirs or something."

"Or something." Dixon took another long swallow of brandy.

"You're not attractive when you're coy, Detective Lloyd."

"I'm getting to it. All in all we brought seventy-three boxes of papers down from Sills's house. It took most of yesterday to load the truck, transport them and then haul them into a conference room at the courthouse."

"Seventy-three boxes. Big ones?"

"Mostly they were those 1.5-cubic-foot boxes that movers use for books."

"Big enough. So what did you find?"

"You know I stayed there all night, right? Got about two hours' sleep on one of the cots at the precinct early this morning."

"Hang on. I'll get my violin."

"Yeah. Bite me. Ninety-nine percent of it was boring stuff. Boxes and boxes of receipts. He must have saved the receipt for every single thing he ever bought. Of the one percent that wasn't boring, the forensics people only gave me what they thought would be relevant to our case, which might have been one percent of one percent."

Ethan sat up and tossed the empty chip bag into the waste can and wiped his hand on his jeans before picking up his cola. "I'm getting the picture. So did the one one-thousandth percent pique your interest?"

Dixon wiped his hand down his face. "A little bit," he muttered. "First. Darby Sills was definitely blackmailing somebody."

Ethan practically did a spit take. "Son of a— Seriously? Who?"

"Damned if I can tell. I wouldn't be surprised if he didn't know himself. His creative accounting is that good."

"Who figured it out? You? One of the forensic guys? Y'all don't have the bank records and safe-deposit box yet, do you?"

"Slow down, Delancey. One of the forensic techs brought me his bank statements this afternoon. She'd started early yesterday and had been studying the deposits all day and night and most of the day today. She's worked out a pattern, but even after she walked me through it twice I still can't find it on my own."

"How much? How long has it been going on? And damn it! Who was he blackmailing?"

"Those are the $64,000 questions. There's a forensic accountant working with our techs right now. I'm hoping he'll have an answer for us soon."

"Could the tech tell how long it had been going on?"

Dixon nodded and Ethan saw a gleam in his eyes. "For the past ten years, according to the accountant."

"Ten years ago. And he put the deposits into his regular account? Man, he had some nerve. They talk about these politicians who think they're untouchable. But Darby Sills took it to a new level. And nobody can figure out who he was blackmailing? Or what the hell some-body did that they'd pay to keep quiet?"

"That's right. I've asked Farrantino to pull any case files from that year and the two years on either side that may have to do with Sills or Buddy Davis. I'm counting on the forensic accountant to find some trace of who Sills's money was coming from."

Ethan thought for a couple of moments. "Maybe you should include Whitley and Stamps. Oh, and get one of those accountants to com-pare their financials with Sills's. See if any-thing in their records matches up."

"Good idea. What about Davis's financials?" Dixon asked.

Ethan laughed. "Sure. Why not. It could be good for a laugh. I can see it now, Buddy and Benita standing there with their lawyer, thumb-ing their noses at us. I'm not sure there's a snowball's chance in hell that we'll ever see a single piece of paper from them."

"We could get a court order."

"I don't know. First hint that we're coming for their records, Benita is liable to start a bonfire that could be seen from space." Ethan paused. "Man, I wish I could deal with Buddy and leave her out of it."

"Why's that?" Dixon asked as he got up to pour himself another few millimeters of brandy.

"He's the polar opposite of Benita. He's easygoing, quiet. Sometimes it seems like he's not even all there. Like he's—"

"Like he's what?"

Ethan frowned. "I don't know. He'll be talking and just sort of drift off."

"Like he's crazy?"

"I don't know. Either there's something wrong with him or he's putting on a hell of an act."

"Why don't you separate the two of them? It's your prerogative as the investigating officer."

"I'm probably going to have to do that. I doubt we'll get the answers we need by investigating them together. But separating them could stir up a whole 'nother hornet's nest. They're big friends with the Superintendent and they'll be in there pulling every string they've got as soon as I even try to put them in separate rooms."

"True," Dixon said on a sigh. He set his snifter down and picked up a manila folder he must have put there when he first came in.

When he sat back down, Ethan said, "What's that?"

"It's the other thing I found," Dixon said. His expression was grim. "I'll let you read it." He slid the folder across the smooth surface of the coffee table.

Ethan caught it before it came to a stop. There

was only one sheet of paper in the folder. He read the entire sheet. At one point, he glanced up briefly to find his partner watching him over tented fingers, then he read the entire sheet again.

The contents were shocking to him, although they probably shouldn't be. Con Delancey had never claimed to be a saint. Although from everything Ethan had heard throughout his life about his grandfather, he would have figured the man to be more discreet and respectful of his wife.

"Where did you get this?" he asked.

"Sills's house. I take it you didn't know. Do you think any of your family does?"

"Know that my grandfather had an affair with Kit Powers, the famous Bourbon Street stripper? Yes. Know that he fathered a son with her? No." Ethan laughed harshly. "I think I can say with a fair measure of certainty that none of the Delanceys know that. If they had, I think I'd have heard."

He looked back at the certified copy of the birth certificate of Joseph Edward Powers, then thumped it with his knuckles. "Did you notice the date? Joseph Powers was born the same year I was. Hell, he's only a month younger than me." Ethan didn't even try to hide the bitterness in his voice.

"From what I've heard—" Dixon started, then stopped.

Ethan sent him a sidelong look. "Go ahead. What were you going to say?"

Dixon shook his head. "Nothing. Forget it." Dixon took a sip of his brandy and swirled the glass, watching the golden liquid.

"Come on, Dix. It's not like you're going to say anything I haven't heard before. You think I don't know what kind of man my grandfather was? I mean, in a lot of ways he was admirable. His record of public service is long and filled with innovative programs to help the people of Louisiana. He was generous—he'd give a man the money in his pocket and did, many, many days. But he was a scoundrel." Ethan gestured toward the birth certificate. "No denying it."

"People say your grandmother locked her bedroom door after their youngest child was born."

"I know. I've heard that." He shrugged. "And maybe it's an excuse for what he did. But—"

Dixon didn't speak.

"He was my granddad. It's hard to think about another Delancey out there. A—what? Half cousin? Plus, if there's one, who's to say there aren't more?" He chuckled wryly. "Dozens even."

After a pause, Dixon spoke. "So what do you want to do about it?"

Ethan sighed and closed the folder and set it on the coffee table. "Hell if I know," he muttered, still unable to take his eyes off the plain folder. "Who all saw this?"

Dixon thought. "Maybe nobody other than the tech who brought me the folder. The only label on it said Delancey. The tech said, 'I thought you might want to go through this yourself.' I suppose I could ask him if he looked at anything."

"No. Leave it alone. I want this under lock and key. Nobody is to know about it."

"Are you sure?"

Ethan nodded. "Until all this mess with Sills's death is over—absolutely. Personally, I'd rather not have this information released—ever. But even thinking as a detective investigating a high-profile murder, I know that this piece of paper will only muddy the waters and cause a flurry of gossip and renewed interest in Con Delancey. We can't afford all that distraction if we're going to find Sills's murderer."

"I agree. The question is, do we give it to the commander or do we keep it secret?"

"My vote? Keep it secret. I'll put it in my safe-deposit box."

Dixon looked at him questioningly. "You don't think that's withholding evidence?"

"Evidence of what?" Ethan said on a laugh. "Con Delancey's wandering…eye?"

Dixon stood. "Okay. It's your family. It's your call. Do you want the rest of the folder?"

"Yeah. I'll stick it all in the box. What's in the rest of it?"

Dixon held up his thumb and forefinger, about an inch apart. "Documentation of meetings Sills had with your grandfather. Later on, cassette tapes. Looks to me like he was hoping to be able to blackmail Con. I haven't listened to the tapes, but as far as written records, that birth certificate was the only thing in the whole file that he could have used. I wonder why he never did."

Ethan stood, too, and held up his hands as if framing a screenshot. "I can see it now. Sills tells Granddad what he's got and Granddad just shrugs and says, 'Slap it on the front page for all I care.' I'll bet that's exactly why it's buried in a dusty file. I'll bet Con Delancey told him where he could put it."

"Well, I'd better get home. I just wanted to tell you about Sills's information on your granddad."

Ethan followed Dixon out onto the porch. "Yeah. I appreciate it. Let me know as soon as you get the safe-deposit box. I'm betting that if there's any information anywhere about the people Sills was blackmailing, it'll be in that box. Once we've got those names, then we'll have a real suspect list."

Chapter Six

It was after four by the time Laney finally got on the road back to New Orleans from Baton Rouge. The meetings had gone longer than she'd anticipated. The first one, to discuss who would be appointed to finish out Senator Sills's term, had deteriorated into a three-hour debate between the governor's executive assistant and the president of the senate. The only thing they agreed on was that Laney should work with the new appointee's staff to ease the transition. They couldn't even agree on who would pay her.

That information, she thought bitterly as she exited off I-10 onto Veterans Memorial Boulevard, could have been passed on to her in a phone call.

The second meeting, to discuss the funeral arrangements, was delayed because the senator's older daughter's baby had an earache. By the time it was over, Laney had been excused from any part in the planning or execution of the funeral by both daughters, who also spent quite a bit of time debating. When four o'clock rolled around and nobody seemed inclined to wrap up the *discussion,* Laney excused herself, saying that she had to get back to New Orleans before dark.

Now she drove to the storage building she'd rented when her dad had gone into an assisted-living facility. At the time, it had seemed like a good idea to rent storage space near his home in Kenner so she could move furniture, boxes and books as she had time. Now she wished she'd gotten one nearer her rented house in the lower Garden District.

She keyed in the password at the gate to the storage facility and drove to her building. By the time she unlocked the padlock on the garage door it was five o'clock, and she needed a flashlight to find the two boxes labeled Dad's Papers and wrestled them into the backseat of her car, probably ruining her dark blue slacks and gray blouse.

As she headed back through the gate and onto the access road for Veterans Memorial Highway, a car appeared out of nowhere and sped straight toward her. She tried to gun the engine to get out of the way, but the other car veered at the last second and sideswiped her on the driver's side.

The screech of metal on metal hurt her ears as the impact sent her car spinning into the other lane, where a panel truck barely missed her. Her car slid sideways off the shoulder of the road and finally came to a stop.

Laney sat unmoving, stunned. From the first instant when she'd seen the small car barreling toward her, everything had moved in slow motion. She'd experienced every second as if she were watching one of those super-slow vignettes in a movie. The kind of split-screen action where the driver relived years of memories in the few seconds it took to crash a car or down a plane.

Vaguely, she became aware of a rapping noise. She opened her eyes and saw a man looking at her through the windshield. He was saying something she couldn't understand. After watching him blankly for a moment, she realized he was motioning for her to roll down her window. She pressed the button on the console, but although she could hear an electrical whirr, nothing happened. Once the man saw that the window wasn't working, he gestured toward the passenger side. With a passing thought that this wasn't the man who had sideswiped her, because he had on a white cap and that man had worn a black hat, she lowered the window on the passenger side.

"—the door." The man was talking to her.

She frowned. Had he said unlock the door? "I don't—" she said in a barely audible croak.

He peered at her searchingly. "Are you injured? Bleeding? I need to see if you're all right. I've called the police."

Call Ethan, she wanted to say, but she couldn't make a sound. There was a lump in her throat that felt as big and hard as a stone. She shook her head no, because she didn't think she was injured. Then she swallowed hard and tried to talk past the stone. "Who—who are you?" she croaked, peering at him sideways. For some reason she thought it might be better if she didn't move too much. She felt slightly nauseated and every time she turned or nodded her head, it seemed as though something hurt somewhere.

"I was in the truck. That car pushed you right into my lane. I barely missed you. Was he chasing you?"

"No," she whispered raggedly. "I'd just come—" at that second, for the life of her she couldn't remember where she'd been. All she remembered was the crash. "Where's my purse?" she asked.

"It's right here." The man pointed at the floor of the passenger seat.

"My phone. Call Ethan. Delancey." She tried to shift in her seat and found out, first, that she couldn't move, and second, that the vague pain she'd noticed had suddenly become very specific and very sharp. "My shoulder hurts," she said.

The man grabbed her purse, then glanced up. "Okay," he said. "Just stay right there. The EMTs are on their way."

It took over twenty minutes for the EMTs to get her out of the car. The damage to the frame wasn't that bad, but the door was bent in enough that it kept the lock on the seat belt from releasing. The EMTs had to pry off the driver's-side door, then cut the seat belt.

They checked her vital signs and carefully examined her for broken bones or internal injuries. Once they were satisfied that her only injury seemed to be a bruised left shoulder from the impact, they got her to her feet and helped her walk to the back of the ambulance and sit.

"Okay," the male EMT said. "How're you doing?"

"I'm feeling kind of sick," she whispered. "Sorry."

"Hey, don't apologize to me," the young EMT said with a little chuckle. He pointed to his female partner. "Just turn your head toward her if you think you're going to throw up, okay?"

WHEN ETHAN GOT to the scene of the accident, he noticed that Detective Stephen Benoit of the Kenner Police Department, whom he'd met a couple of times before, seemed to be in charge. He quickly introduced himself, in case the other man didn't remember him, and explained that the accident could be connected with a case of his and that Laney Montgomery was his witness and a victim in the crime. Benoit gave him a quick rundown of what had happened and told him to stick with him. A crime scene tech came up to the detective, so

Ethan took a few steps closer to the back of the ambulance, so that he could see where Laney was sitting.

She seemed unhurt, he saw with relief, except for her left shoulder, which one of the EMTs was carefully manipulating.

From what he could hear of their conversation, the EMT was explaining about the bruised biceps and triceps and what she could expect. Each time he appeared to be finished, Laney would ask another question. Once the EMT tried to brush off her questions, saying the answer was just a bunch of technical stuff that she didn't need to know.

"I do," she said earnestly. "Please. I need to understand."

The EMT patiently explained about bruises and how ice was the best thing for a fresh bruise. As he talked to her, the other EMT taped a reusable ice pack to her shoulder on top of her blouse.

Ethan knew that a couple of hours spent with her did not make him an expert on Laney Montgomery, but right now, watching her as she concentrated on what the EMT was telling her, he was certainly getting a more complete picture of her. She'd been precise and careful in her answers to his questions about the shooting, but now it occurred to him that she was just as precise and step-by-step about everything.

He allowed himself a small smile. He understood, maybe better than a lot of people ever could, where all that need for precision came from. It was her effort to hold on to as much control as she could, even in situations where no control was possible, like right now. He could identify with that. Living in the same house as his father and his oldest brother Lucas, who were always at loggerheads, he'd learned before age ten that logic and careful attention to facts got him a lot further than an explosive temper and a short fuse. He wondered what in her life had taught Laney that lesson. He could see that she was more of a control freak than he was.

It didn't take much imagination to see that she would be hell to live with. But the question was, would she be worth it? *Oh, yeah.*

Detective Benoit stepped up beside Ethan. "How is she?" he asked.

"Looks like just a bruised arm," Ethan said. "Mostly she's just shaken up. You talked with the guy driving the truck?"

Benoit nodded. "He saw the vehicle speed toward Ms. Montgomery's car. Said he heard the engine rev. The car was definitely gaining speed. It was no accident."

"Did he see anything?"

Benoit nodded. "Definitely. The vehicle was

a sports car. Red, naturally. He didn't know the make. Said it was one of those low, fast things. Maybe Italian. He caught a glimpse of the license plate."

"He did?" Ethan was excited. Maybe he could get a lead on Sills's murderer from this.

"Only got two letters and he's not sure of the position of the letters or color or state. But he swears the two letters are correct. He also saw the driver. Said the man had on a black cowboy hat with some kind of shiny decoration on it."

Black cowboy hat with shiny things. Ethan grabbed his pad and made a note. "What were the two letters the driver saw?"

Benoit consulted his own notes. "C and F."

Ethan wrote that down as his brain fed him the obvious interpretation of that partial plate—something to do with Circle of Faith. "I need to run Buddy Davis's plates. I know he drives a sports car."

"Why Davis?" Benoit asked.

"Something the witness told us about the man who shot the senator and her. The C and the F on the license could be 'Circle of Faith.'"

Benoit gave him a skeptical look.

"Look, man," Ethan said. "I hate that I can't be more specific, but my commander wants us to keep certain things under wraps."

"No problem," Benoit said.

Out of the corner of his eye, Ethan saw the EMT hand Laney a little plastic bag with two tablets in it.

She nodded. "Thank you," she said, her voice breaking.

He glanced at Benoit, who nodded. So he stepped closer to her. "Hey," he said with a smile as the EMT closed his emergency box and moved out of the way. "It's all over now. You're fine."

"You came," she said, her voice quivering slightly.

"Of course I did," he responded. Obviously she was a lot more shaken than she appeared to be. Although she'd been at the point of tears several times, she hadn't actually cried during the entire ordeal the other night. That probably explained her tears now. She'd been through a lot and now she'd reached her breaking point.

He didn't want to take a chance on making it worse, so he took a deep breath and put on his "just the facts ma'am" demeanor, figuring that would be better than being too nice or too solicitous. As much as she valued her control, she might not be able to keep from crying. "You're my witness. That means you're my responsibility."

She sniffed, bit her lip, then nodded.

Benoit stepped up and began questioning her, writing down everything she told him. Once he was done, he said, "We'll need to get you back over here to read and sign your statement, Ms. Montgomery."

Ethan spoke up. "If you'll send it over to the Eighth, I'll make sure it's signed and sent back."

Benoit agreed. He thanked Laney and him and told her that one of his officers could take her home.

"That's okay. I'll take her," Ethan said. "Let me ask you a favor. She told you she'd stopped at the mini-storage to pick up some boxes. They're right there in the backseat of her car. She picked them up because they're part of my investigation into the murder of Senator Darby Sills."

He heard a murmur of protest from Laney, but ignored it as he saw the detective's eyes widen. "That's the case you're working on? I thought I recognized the name Montgomery."

Ethan nodded. "I need to take them with me."

"Technically, those boxes are part of this incident."

Ethan grimaced internally. "Technically," he said with a nod, "you're right. I'd owe you one."

The detective regarded him thoughtfully for a moment. "Send me an official request first thing tomorrow," he said.

Ethan nodded. "First thing." He held his breath. He wanted the boxes tonight. If he was right, they were Elliott Montgomery's personal financial records. They might include proof that Darby Sills was blackmailing him.

"Okay," the detective said, nodding. "Go ahead and take them. Need any help?"

Ethan shook his head. "Thanks." He shook the detective's hand again, then got the keys to the car from the tow truck driver and quickly transferred two medium-size boxes from Laney's backseat to his trunk.

While he was doing that, Laney stood and waved off a police officer's help. She walked over to his car. Her eyes still sparkled with unshed tears as she faced him, her back straight, her face flushed with anger. The effect was diminished by the pale blue sling the EMTs had given her for her arm. "You can't possibly believe that my father was being blackmailed."

"So you eavesdropped on my conversation with the detective."

"Of course I did. It concerned me. How could you possibly think Senator Sills was blackmailing *my* father. Go after the dozens and dozens of people Sills *could* have something on."

"Seems to me that Elliott Montgomery could be one of them. And you know I'm checking out everybody who had a relationship with Sills. Tell me something, Laney. Why did you want those boxes, anyhow, if it wasn't to see if his bank statements showed excessive with-drawals?"

Laney stared at him, fury blazing in her blue eyes. "I don't have to answer that," she said. "They are my property, and I don't think you can just *confiscate* them."

"On the side of the boxes it says 'Dad's Papers.' I was going to ask you for them anyway," he said, opening the passenger door for her.

"That does not answer my question," she said icily.

He looked at her. "Let me refer again to the discussion I just had with the other detective."

She scowled. "What about it?"

"There's the answer to your question. I can take those boxes, and I did."

"But the way you told that detective, you let him think I was getting the boxes for you. What if I tell him I wasn't? Don't you need a search warrant or a court order or something?"

He shook his head. "They were in plain sight. Sorry."

She sent him a scathing look, then carefully got into his car and reached for the seat belt, pausing when she realized she couldn't fasten it with her arm in a sling. "I don't see why I have to wear this ridiculous thing. My shoulder isn't bothering me that much."

Ethan noticed her struggle. He said, "Hang on. I'll get it for you." He closed the passenger door and went around to get in on the driver's side. As he reached across her for the belt, he caught a whiff of something sweet and citrusy. Unable to help himself, he turned his head slightly to breathe in the scent. A soft, choked sound came from her.

Embarrassed, he pulled back immediately, pulling the seat belt with him and quickly attaching it. "Sorry," he said, starting the car as he glanced sidelong at her.

Her right arm came across her middle to cradle the wrapped left arm. She cleared her throat. "Detective?"

"It's Ethan," he said gruffly.

"I don't want you looking in those boxes until I've had a chance to go through everything."

He glanced over at her. "We can look at them together."

"No."

"Then I'll take them to the station and you won't get to see them at all until this case is over."

She sniffed in exasperation and leaned her head back against the headrest. He could feel frustration and anger emanating from her in waves.

"Sorry," he said for about the third time since he'd gotten to the accident scene. "I'm not just being mean. And you don't have the authority to *allow* me to see the contents of those boxes.

This is a murder investigation. Your dad's papers are evidence. If I can find out who Darby Sills was blackmailing, I'll be that much closer to the killer."

After a moment of dead silence, Laney said, "Well, I can tell you for a fact that my father didn't kill Senator Sills."

"That *is* a fact," he said carefully. "Indisputable, since your father is dead."

"Oh, my God, do you think I killed the senator?"

"No—"

"You do. Pretty clever, huh? Shooting myself. Wait a minute. The crime scene techs checked my hands for gunshot residue, didn't they? Have you figured out how I managed to graze my temple without getting powder burns on my face or gunshot residue on my hands? Well, let me just tell you right now. I am that good."

He heard the pain and fear behind her angry words. "You know," he said. "You're allowed to be upset. You're even allowed to be scared. A lot has happened to you in a short time."

"Don't patronize me, *Detective*. I am perfectly capable of handling things. But the very idea that you could think I had anything to do with the senator's murder—" Her voice caught. She cleared her throat, trying to cover it, but he wasn't fooled. If he looked at her right now, he knew that he'd see tears in her eyes again.

"So you can *handle things* when someone is murdered practically in front of you, you're shot and two days later you're rammed by a car?"

"Yes," she said. She tried for a determined, confident answer, but her voice was meek.

"Well, you're doing a great job," he said as he pulled up to the curb in front of her house. He jumped out of the car and went around to open the passenger door. He held out his hand but Laney ignored it, climbed out awkwardly.

"Don't bother walking me to my door," she said. "I'll be just fine."

"Will you?" he asked as he closed the car door. "Okay, tell me this. Are you going to take those tablets the EMT gave you?"

"I haven't decided yet."

"Have you got someone coming to stay with you tonight?"

"Why in the world would I need anyone to stay with me?" she asked.

When she fished her keys out of her purse, he took them from her and unlocked the door. He stepped inside and flipped on the lights, then examined her face. "You're pale. You look like you're about to pass out. Is your arm hurting?"

"A few bruises never bother gorgeous cops on TV."

Ethan glanced at her in amusement. "The important word there is *TV.* Again—fiction."

"Fine," she said. She'd never realized how difficult it was to deal with a purely logical mind. She'd always been the most practical person she knew. But Ethan Delancey had her beat by a mile. Several miles.

"I have ibuprofen in that cabinet with the coffee cups." She gestured. "There's cranberry juice in the refrigerator. I'd like half juice and half water. No ice. But if you want something to drink, you can probably figure out where the ice is. I'm going to sit down in the living room. I'm feeling a little woozy."

She sat down on the couch that had been her dad's and did her best not to cry. She was upset. She was scared. Her shoulder hurt. And in a couple of hours, Detective Ethan Delancey would know as much about her father and his dealings as she did. And it was entirely possible that she herself would know more than she ever wanted to know about the man who'd raised her alone after his wife, her mother, died of alcohol poisoning.

"I'm going to get the boxes and bring them inside," Ethan said.

Laney clenched her fists as the front door banged against the wall of her foyer. She aimed a scathing look toward the door, but truthfully, she was more angry at herself. "I should have put the them in my trunk," she muttered. If she'd taken the extra trouble then, Ethan wouldn't have seen them and she wouldn't be torn between two choices—looking at her father's papers in front of a detective or relinquishing them to the police. In either case, she probably wouldn't get them back for years.

But at least if she looked at them here with Ethan, she'd know what was in them.

Chapter Seven

Laney yawned and tried to focus on the bank statement she was holding. She was having trouble keeping her eyes open. "What's wrong?" Ethan asked. He was sitting on the floor with his back against the couch, sorting through papers.

She looked up bleary-eyed. "What?"

"You groaned."

"No I didn't," she said, although she knew he was right.

"You're about to fall asleep, aren't you? You should go to bed."

"I'm not going anywhere and leaving you to go through my dad's stuff alone."

"Don't trust me?"

"Not as far as I could throw you if you were holding both boxes," she said, trying to suppress a yawn.

"Are you hungry? What have you eaten today?"

Laney opened her mouth to answer, but stopped. She couldn't remember. She'd drunk a cup of awful coffee at the precinct early in the morning and had a couple of glasses of water during the day, but food?

"You haven't eaten, have you? I knew it. I'm hungry, too."

She thought about the pasta she'd never made the night before and her mouth watered. "I can make spinach pasta," she said, then looked down at the sling on her left arm. "Or I could if I had two arms."

Ethan rose to his feet. "I have two arms. I can make it if it's not too hard."

She stood, too, and stretched. "It's not hard at all. Butter, garlic, frozen spinach, mascarpone cheese and Parmesan. Come on. We need to get the water boiling for the spaghetti." She led the way into the kitchen. When she turned, Ethan was way too close to her.

Her little kitchen, which she'd always thought of as cozy and comfortable, suddenly seemed as small as a broom closet, with him standing there, towering over her by at least five inches.

He smiled. "What's the catch?"

"The catch?"

"With the pasta sauce? It can't be as easy as it sounds."

She slid past him to open the refrigerator, doing her best to ignore his faint clean scent. "There's a package of angel hair pasta in that cabinet next to the sink, and there's a big pot in the cabinet below the counter." Her voice sounded stiff to her ears, and higher pitched than usual. She cleared her throat as she pulled the thawed spinach, cheeses and butter out of the refrigerator one at a time.

"There's no catch. Trust me, the sauce is just as easy as it sounds," she said, answering his question. "My mother used to make it back before—" She stopped, then went on quickly, trying to cover what she'd almost said. *Back before she died from drinking.* "She always said it was a perfect date dinner. Said my father proposed over a big plate of her spinach pasta."

While she'd been talking, Ethan had retrieved the pot and filled it with water. He set it on the stove and turned on the gas. Then he looked at her. "Perfect date dinner? Good to know."

Before she could interpret the look he'd sent her way, he turned and grabbed a package of angel hair pasta from the cabinet. "This won't take long to cook," he said.

Laney set a skillet on the stove and awkwardly unwrapped a stick of butter, one-handed. With a knife, she cut half off and put it in the skillet. "Sounds like you know a little bit about cooking."

"My dorm mates and I ate a lot of spaghetti and Tony Chachere's in college."

"Tony's? That's all you put on it?"

"Don't knock it. It's pretty good if you're trying to eat cheap."

Laney grabbed a jar of minced garlic from the refrigerator. She set it on the counter and tried to slide the sling back so she could hold it with her left hand. "Okay, that does it," she muttered. "This thing's coming off." She reached behind her head, looking for the fastener.

"Hey, what are you doing?" Ethan said. "Give

me that jar." He opened the jar for her and she put a heaping teaspoonful in the melted butter.

"That's a lot of garlic," he said.

"If you don't like it I might have some Tony's," she retorted.

He laughed. Unlike his smiles and smirks, his laugh was hearty and genuine. When she glanced up, his mouth was stretched wide and, she noticed with surprise, he did have laugh lines. They, along with his dark, serious eyes, were just about the only thing that kept him from looking like a teenager instead of a police detective who had to be in his early thirties. She felt laughter bubbling up from inside her. It had been days since she'd even felt like smiling, much less laughing.

She picked up the container of mascarpone cheese and tried to pry the top off, but with one hand, it was impossible. She growled.

Ethan reached over and put his hand on top

of hers. "Hey," he said. "I've got all this. Don't get so frustrated." He opened the container. "How much?"

"All of it."

He emptied it into the skillet as she stirred. "Man, that smells amazing."

"It is amazing," she said. The bowl of drained spinach was covered with plastic wrap, which she managed to pull off with one hand. She dumped it into the skillet and began stirring everything with the tongs.

"Should I put the pasta in the water?" he asked. "It's about to boil."

"Sure. The sauce will be ready in about seven minutes or so. That should be just about perfect timing."

By the time Ethan drained the angel hair, the spinach mixture was creamy and hot. She added a generous pinch of salt and handed Ethan the pepper grinder.

"About three turns ought to be good," she said.

He turned the pepper grinder, then leaned over the skillet to take a deep whiff. "Wow. Is it ready?"

She nodded, grinning at him. "Except for the Parmesan." He twisted off the cap for her and she added a generous portion to the mixture. "Now, pour the spinach sauce over the pasta and mix it, please?"

"Yes, ma'am." He picked up the skillet and poured the sauce into the pot of drained angel hair pasta. Then using the tongs, he tossed the two together quickly. He turned to her with raised brows. "*Now* is it ready?"

She laughed at his boyish question as she reached into a cabinet and came out with two bowls. "Dish us up some and I'll grab the jar of Parmesan in case we need more, although I don't think we will."

Within a minute they were sitting at her small dining room table and eating. "I have some wine," she said. "But—"

"Yeah. Better not. You realize we're only about halfway through the boxes."

"I do," Laney said, "but the good news is I found Dad's bank statements."

"Good, because what I've been sifting through are tax records and receipts from back in the nineties. When we finish eating, I'll take some of those bank statements, because that's where any indication of blackmail is going to be." He gestured with his fork. "This is spectacular," he said. "I can see why your dad proposed."

"It's magical food," she said, smiling, too, as she shoved another forkful into her mouth. Tonight Ethan reminded her of how he'd been when he'd come to see her in the E.R. Gentle, kind and solicitous. But after his officious attitude in the interview room at the precinct, she'd decided the pain medication had made her dream that he'd been nice. Still, she could definitely understand why people talked about the Delancey charm, not to mention the Delancey good looks.

Ethan had on a white shirt, dress pants and leather loafers that would probably decimate her salary. It was the same uniform he wore at work, minus the sports jacket, but somehow tonight he seemed like just a guy, instead of a logic-driven, uptight police detective, concerned with *just the facts, ma'am.*

In fact, he seemed like the kind of guy she'd always wanted to meet. Intelligent, considerate, funny. *Whoa.* Was she actually thinking about Ethan Delancey as a man she could date? She felt her face grow warm. She didn't want him to ask her why she was blushing, so she stood to carry her bowl to the kitchen.

"Don't even think about trying to do the dishes. I'll take care of them." He stood and picked up his bowl.

"I'll let you. Isn't it time to take the ice pack off my arm?"

"Probably. How does it feel?"

"Hard to say. It's numb." She flexed it gingerly. "It's not as sore, though. Can you take it off?" She turned her back and held her hair out of the way.

When he touched her neck as he worked the ice pack out from under the sling, she shivered. His fingers were hot against her chilled skin, and she wondered if they would feel just as hot and make her just as tingly if he touched her in other, more intimate places.

"Got it," he said and stepped around her to put it in the freezer.

She had to swallow before she could speak.

"Thanks. I'm going to go back to the papers and leave you alone with the kitchen cleanup."

"Are you sure you're up for more sifting through piles?" he asked. "It's after eight. You might want to take one of those tablets and head to bed. The EMT said to rest."

Laney stared at him. "Go to bed? At eight o'clock? I don't think so."

"See. You're already going against doctor's orders. You sleep and I'll finish going through the papers, then sack out on the couch."

"Sack out—? Why?"

"Because somebody's got to watch over you while you're incapacitated."

"I'm not incapacitated. It's just a bruise and I am not going to sleep in a sling. And I'm sure not going to bed in the middle of the evening."

"See. I can't leave. I've got to make sure you follow doctor's orders."

"What you'll do is go through the papers

and then go home," she said, angling a disgusted look at him as she headed back to the living room. Sitting down on the couch, she picked up the small pile of papers she'd been going through earlier. From the kitchen came the sound of water running and dishes rattling. She shook her head at the image of Police Detective Ethan Delancey washing her dishes.

Being nice and charming was one thing, but why was he talking about spending the night on her couch? She'd seen in his face that he knew the excuse of watching over her was ridiculous. But what was his real reason? She didn't know, but she wasn't comfortable with it, whatever it was. She knew she wouldn't be able to sleep if he were out here on the couch. She'd lie awake knowing there was no way in hell he and she would ever get together, but wishing he was in her bed anyway.

Doing her best to shake off the picture of him

lying on her couch in his shorts—or briefs, she picked up the first folded and rubber-banded pack of bank statements. She opened it and perused the first sheet. It was for the month of January, a year before her dad had died. It looked like she'd expected it to. Deposits, the monthly fee for the assisted-living facility, automatic payments for utilities and insurance, and cash withdrawals. Nothing unusual. She smiled wistfully as she looked at the withdrawals. He liked to play the slot machines, and went to Harrah's casino near the Riverwalk once or twice a week. She'd often met him there or at a nearby restaurant for dinner.

She paged through the rest of the statements in the stack, which could almost be photocopies of the January one. With a sigh, she wrapped the rubber band around them and set them aside. Then she pulled eleven identical packets out of the box. There they were. Twelve years' worth of Elliott Montgomery's day-to-day life.

Ethan came back into the room as she was dumping the packets onto the floor and delving back into the box.

"What's all that?" he asked.

"A dozen years of my dad's life," she answered, her voice breaking. "I never thought that checking account statements would be personal, but I can see his everyday life by looking at those sheets." She felt her eyes fill with tears and blinked them away before Ethan could see how sentimental she was.

"You're saying there's nothing unusual. Nothing you wouldn't expect. Withdrawals? Checks?"

"That's right. All those statements, and there's probably only a few dollars' difference between one and the next."

"So that's checking and savings?"

She stopped. "Savings," she said, looking up at him. "Savings. Oh, my God." She started pulling papers out of the box. "I can't believe I didn't remember. After he died, I was surprised at how little money he had in savings."

Ethan's gaze sharpened. "Why?"

"He used to talk about the bonuses he would get from various companies at the end of the year—for doing a good job lobbying for them." She shook her head. "When he went into the assisted-living community, we thought it would take everything he had to buy into it. Luckily, we were able to sell his house and that almost paid for the buy-in. His monthly rent came out of his checking account, just like his mortgage did in earlier years. But all that money that should have been left in his savings account—wasn't there."

"How much are you talking about?"

Laney hesitated. She'd learned a long time

ago that most people were suspicious of lob-byists anyway. When—if she told Ethan how much money her father had saved, what would he say?

He met her gaze and she knew he'd picked up on her hesitation and the reason for it. "Laney, my grandfather was Con Delancey. I'm not going to pass judgment on your dad for what he did for a living or how much money he amassed doing it. All I want to know is how much money went missing from his savings account and when it happened."

"He went into the assisted-living commu-nity six years ago. I have no idea how much money he'd put into savings during his life, but at the time we were calculating how much it would cost for him to live there, his balance was around three hundred thousand— No."

She shook her head, not even able to allow the next thought into her head. "I don't believe my dad was being blackmailed. He would never have done anything he was that desperate to hide."

"How much was in the account when he died?"

"I—" she said, then had to swallow the acrid saliva that rose in her throat. The answer to that question made her nauseous.

"Laney? How much?"

"Around twenty thousand." She could barely speak the words. "I wondered what had happened to the money, but I never even thought about—" She definitely couldn't say that word in connection with her dad.

"Wow," Ethan said. "In six years. That's fifty thousand a year over and above his daily expenses. Was he that big a gambler?"

Laney laughed uneasily. "No. I've never known him to take more than a couple hundred into the casino, and if he lost that, he was done for the day."

"Where are the savings records?" Ethan asked.

"I don't know, but I can't believe that—" A thought occurred to her. "Maybe he left it to some charity—anonymously. I wouldn't know about that, right?"

Ethan shook his head. "I'm pretty sure you would. We need to find those records."

Laney sat there.

"Hey," Ethan said, putting a hand on her arm. "Are you all right?"

She shook her head. "I don't want to find the savings records," she said in a small voice. "I don't want to know what happened to that money. Please, can we stop looking?" She looked up at him and saw an odd expression in his eyes. It looked almost pitying.

"No, we can't. I can't. I'll take them to the

precinct and finish there, but I can't stop looking. We know Sills was blackmailing someone.
This is murder, Laney. Murder."

"Well, my dad didn't do it!" she cried. There
were too many awful emotions churning inside
her. Anger, fear, grief, denial.

Ethan took her hand. "Your dad's records
might help us find the killer. I understand how
much it hurts to find out something shocking
about your family. Something you never knew,
and that you can't believe they would do."

"Do you?" she said, pulling her hand away,
but Ethan wouldn't let it go.

He took her other hand, too. "Yes. I found
out, and I managed to live with it. You'll live
with it, too. And if you know your dad, and I'm
sure that you do, you'll find out why he did it,
and you'll be able to live with that, too."

"I'm afraid of knowing," she muttered.

"I know you are." He sat there, holding her hands and looking into her eyes.

She saw them turn smoky and dark and she felt as if she were sinking into their inky depths.

He let go of her hand and touched her cheek. For an instant, she thought he was going to kiss her and she realized she wanted him to. Desperately. She looked down at his mouth.

"Okay?" he whispered.

To kiss me? "Okay," she responded.

"Good." He let go and turned back to the boxes, leaving Laney stunned and embarrassed.

She'd been expecting a sweet, gentle kiss to go with Ethan's sweet, gentle words and touch. But all he'd wanted to do was get back to searching for proof that her father had been being blackmailed.

"Let's keep going," he said. "We don't really have a lot left to go through."

She should have known. Sure, he was charming and good looking. And those qualities obviously worked to his advantage when he wanted something—like now. What a chump she was, to think he'd wanted anything else.

She cleared her throat. "Okay," she said wryly. "Let's."

They dug through the rest of the papers, looking at everything. Laney quickly emptied her box, finding nothing. No bank book. No statements. No records of any kind. "That's impossible, isn't it?" she asked Ethan, doing her best to be a trouper. "There has to be some kind of record of withdrawals from savings."

He nodded, not looking up. "Definitely some kind. I suppose he could have thrown them away, or it could have been totally digital. Did your dad have a laptop computer?"

"No. Dad never advanced into the digital age. He never even had a cell phone."

Ethan picked up a large stack of medical bills and statements.

Laney peeked at a couple. "Those are from ten years ago. When he had his first heart attack and had a triple bypass," she said.

"Wait a second," Ethan said, setting aside the sheets. "There's something else here—" He pulled out a small stack of letters, bound with a rubber band. "What's all this? Letters to your dad from you. Where were you writing from? Summer camp?"

"Let me see those," Laney said. "The only time I went to camp was the year I was thirteen. And I for sure didn't write all those letters." She took the rubber band off and looked at the envelopes. "The top two are the only ones I wrote. These others are—wait. They're in Dad's handwriting. What was he doing, writing on envelopes as if they were from me? Why would he do that?"

She pulled the folded stacks of paper from one of the envelopes. "Oh, my God, Ethan! It's the savings account records. He hid them in here." She quickly read through the top one and her throat closed. She covered her mouth with her hand.

"What's wrong?" Ethan asked.

She shook her head, unable to talk. She held out the folded sheets for him to take.

Ethan saw how upset Laney was. And he was sure he knew why. He took the statement from her and perused it. "Hand me the others," he said, and scanned them, as well. Then he looked up at her, and saw her read the truth in his eyes.

"It's true, isn't it?" she said hoarsely.

He could tell by the look in her eyes that she already knew the answer. She was already thinking it herself. Only she was trying to pretend she wasn't. He knew her brain was spinning, had been ever since she'd remembered the ending balance in the savings account, trying to come up with another plausible explanation for those large withdrawals.

He clenched his jaw. He had to say it, because otherwise she would just sit there for who knew how long, doing her best to deny it. "It's true," he said flatly, figuring that if he tried to comfort her right now, she'd lose it. "Given the size of the withdrawals and the frequency, I don't think there's any doubt."

She swallowed and her gaze wavered, but she didn't say anything.

"Laney, of course your dad was being blackmailed. It's the only explanation."

For a few seconds, she didn't move. Then she folded her hands in her lap as her head moved slowly back and forth, back and forth. "What could he have done? He was a good man. A decent man. He raised me by himself after my mother died."

"People can be blackmailed about all sorts of things, Laney. I just found out that Darby Sills tried to blackmail my grandfather about having a child with another woman. That was hard for me to take. That my grandfather disrespected my grandmother. That there's a Delancey out there that my family has never known about."

"That's *your* family. Everybody knows Con Delancey was a rounder and a crooked politician—" Her hand flew to her mouth again. "Oh, Ethan. I'm sorry. I didn't mean to—"

He waved away her apology. "Don't worry about it. If you knew half the things I know about my family—"

She looked at her hands. "I really believed we wouldn't find anything."

Ethan didn't respond to that directly. "There are some huge withdrawals here."

She nodded, seeming to rally a little. "And he obviously went to a lot of trouble to hide the savings account statements."

"Maybe he was embarrassed, or didn't want you asking questions about where the money went?"

"No. I don't think that's it. Look how he printed his name and address and put my name as the return address. That might fool somebody else, but not me," Laney said, her voice unsteady. "He probably meant for me to find these right after he died. I guess I wasn't paying attention when I packed these, or else I was distracted and didn't stop to think that this bundle was way too big to hold the four or five letters I'd written to him."

Ethan sat down beside Laney and took the statements from her hand, sorted through them quickly, then handed her back about two-thirds of them, starting with the most recent dates. "How many years' worth are here?" he asked.

"Twelve years," she answered. "I'm surprised it isn't forty. He saved just about everything."

"Do you feel like taking these and flagging the inordinately large withdrawals on each statement?" he asked, watching her carefully. Although she was extremely intelligent and highly intuitive, he knew that the little girl inside her that still missed her daddy had just received a huge, agonizingly painful dose of reality about the man who'd reared her.

"Sure," she said, straightening her back. "Do you think, if the withdrawals are blackmail, that he was paying them to Senator Sills?"

"I don't know, but once we have the information about the withdrawals, the forensic accountants can compare them with deposits Sills made. So while you flag those, I'm going to find when the withdrawals started."

It took them over an hour to skim through the monthly statements. As Ethan finished with each year he had, he handed the bundle to Laney. Once he got through ten years of statements and started on the eleventh, he discovered exactly when the withdrawals started. So he bundled the oldest two years up and tossed them back in the box. Laney was still reviewing and flagging. She'd slipped her hand out of the sling so that the job was a little easier.

While she worked, Ethan got up and retrieved the ice pack from the freezer. It was almost frozen.

"Is it time for that again?" Laney asked when she saw him with it.

"You're wincing whenever you move that arm. Here, let me put it under the sling." He stepped up behind her and brushed her hair away from her neck so he could slip the ice pack under the sling without getting it tangled in the strands. When he did, she inclined her head slightly and that sweet, citrusy smell he'd noticed in the car wafted across his nostrils.

To his embarrassment, he felt a pleasant stirring deep inside him that heralded the beginnings of arousal. He tightened his jaw as he made sure the ice pack was secure.

He would not give in to his body's cravings. Not with her. She was a victim, a witness, and tonight, she was a grieving daughter and, last but not least, his responsibility. He turned and went into the kitchen and drew a glass of water from her refrigerator dispenser. It was cold and refreshing as he swallowed it. It would be good if he had another ice pack, one he could apply directly to the area that was fast becoming hot and hard, but the thought was nearly as good as the deed. By the time he'd finished drinking the water, the problem was almost gone.

"Ethan?" Laney called.

With a grimace and a stern, if short, lecture about keeping business and personal stuff separate, he went back into the living room.

"I'm done," she said, gesturing toward the stack of statements on her lap. There were tiny, colored sticky flags adorning every single sheet.

"Are you okay?" he asked. She looked better than she had earlier. The color that had drained from her cheeks was back.

"I am. I'm not sure why. Maybe I'll collapse in grief tomorrow, but right now, I'm kind of creepily fascinated with the amounts of money he withdrew." She shook her head. "Is that awful?"

He smiled. "No. I think your brain is coping by becoming involved with the mundane stuff, the numbers and amounts of withdrawals. Just go with it."

"Okay. So you won't believe how many withdrawals I found. I looked for those over five hundred dollars, because I don't think Dad ever withdrew that much for his personal use. Maybe once or twice, if ever."

"How many?"

"You handed me ten years of statements, so that's essentially 520 weeks, right? Well, he sometimes made withdrawals more than once a week. I counted 848 withdrawals of $500 or more during that ten years."

"Five hundred dollars or more. How much more?"

"Some were as much as a thousand. A few were even larger. Plus, he transferred money from savings to checking a few times a year, usually around $5,000." She rubbed her temple. "I'm still just stunned. I'm sitting here looking at these withdrawals and I still can hardly believe that *my dad* did this."

"I'm going to use the calculator on my phone. Go through the statements and call out the amounts. You can go as fast as you want."

Laney sighed. "That's a lot of numbers. I'm cross-eyed already."

"It won't take too long."

She went through the statements, reading off numbers as rapidly as she could find the flagged entries. "Eight hundred. Sixteen fifty. And seven forty," she said finally. "That's it."

Ethan held up the total. "I can't guarantee I got every single one, but take a look at this. Over $550,000 in ten years."

She pressed her lips together and sent her gaze skyward. He knew the information was devastating to her. After a second, she nodded. "That's probably right," she said. "Your forensic accountants can get the real numbers, can't they?"

Ethan nodded, feeling an unexpected pride in her for rallying, despite the shocking truth that her father was paying blackmail. "Yep. I just wish we had some way of knowing who he was paying. All my instincts say Darby Sills." He paused before asking the question that was on his lips.

"Are you sure you can't imagine what your dad's secret might have been? Nothing sticks out in your mind about your dad and money? Or the relationship between him and Sills?" As he spoke, he stacked the statements and tapped them against the surface of the coffee table to straighten them. Then he picked up the envelopes and a large rubber band.

"No. Dad never talked about money with me. Not after my mother died. The two of them had huge fights about money before she got sick enough that she didn't care to fight about any- thing." She sighed. "It's no wonder he avoided the subject at all costs."

"You've mentioned your mother a couple of times. Did she die when you were young?"

Laney nodded. She bit her lip for a second, then sighed. "You should probably know every- thing, if my father's information can help with finding out who murdered Senator Sills. My mother was an alcoholic. A very good one," she said with a sad smile. "Apparently she could drink a lot without actually appearing drunk, until she passed out."

"I'm sorry, Laney."

"And that's what killed her. She died when I was eleven. I know most of this because he told me. She was hiding vodka and drinking about a quart a day. I know—" she said, holding up a hand. "That's hard to believe. Most days by the time Dad got home, she was passed out."

"But what about you?" Ethan interjected.

"I was pretty good at taking care of myself. But one day when she left the stove on and I burned myself trying to turn it off, Dad decided she had to get help. He made her go to rehab. She stayed for about two weeks and was not drinking. But she checked herself out, went to a hotel, drank a quart of vodka and died of alcohol poisoning. It was probably a wonder that she hadn't overdosed before then."

Ethan looked down at the bank statements. Now he knew. Now he understood. Laney had been forced into the role of adult. Her father had worked and she'd been at home with her mother, after school and in the summer. And so, she'd become an adult, probably a long time before the age of eleven. No wonder she never answered a question on the fly. No wonder she assessed everyone. Children of alcoholics have a warped sense of trust, if they can trust at all.

He understood that because of his father, who had been a mean and violent drunk before his stroke.

"I'm so sorry," he said, not only because of how her mother had died, but also because of how her mother had forced her to live.

"I'm good," she said. "I've done a pretty good job of getting over all that. But thanks."

He nodded. She had done a good job. An excellent job.

She pushed her hair back and stretched and yawned. "So you mentioned earlier about my dad's relationship with Senator Sills."

"Right," he said. "I did."

"All I ever knew about Senator Sills was that he and Dad had known each other forever, and about once a month or so, Sills would come over to the house and he and Dad would sit in the living room with the door closed." She stopped for a moment. "I *do* remember them yelling at each other. But I was a teenager and all I wanted to do was listen to music, so I pretty much stayed in my room with my stereo turned up."

"Their meetings could be a clue. Maybe your dad made the withdrawals and then Sills came by once a month to get the money." As he spoke, he stretched the rubber band around the statements and envelopes. When he did, a scrap of paper fell out.

Laney bent down to pick it up. "Something fell out," she said, looking at the small piece of paper. "It looks like one of Dad's notes. He was always writing me notes on torn scraps—" She gasped. "Oh, Dad."

Ethan saw her face crumple. "What is it? What's on the piece of paper?"

She handed it to him without looking up. She pressed her right hand against her mouth, trying not to sob.

Ethan looked at the scribbled note. The first line read, "I hope you find this, daughter. First thing, get away from Darby Sills. He's dangerous."

Chapter Eight

Ethan read the first line again, then the rest of the note.

> I hope you find this, daughter. First thing, get away from Darby Sills. He's dangerous. Quit that job and don't go back. Take this note and the savings account statements to the police. Make sure they know how dangerous Darby is. And make sure you get all the money back. It was always meant for you.

"Meant for me," she said through her tears. "Oh—" She sniffed, then bent her head and covered her eyes with her good hand.

"Hey," Ethan said softly. "It's okay."

She shook her head. "He meant the money for me," she wailed. "He was trying to take care of me and Darby Sills stole everything—" Her voice gave out and she began to cry.

Ethan had no idea what to do. Laney's heart was broken, not only because of what Sills had done to her dad, but also because she'd just discovered that her father wasn't the superhero and saint that she'd believed him to be.

For Ethan, as soon as he heard what was in the note, his first instinct had been to grab it and the bank records and rush down to the courthouse where the forensic accountants were working. By morning they could have the withdrawal amounts matched up with Sills's deposits. Because as well-meaning as Laney's father had been, he hadn't actually written anything in the note that Ethan could use to prove that Sills was blackmailing him.

But looking at Laney, he knew he couldn't just grab her dad's records away from her and leave. She needed comfort and reassurance right now, and as much as he dreaded having to offer her comfort, knowing what it was going to do to him to be that close to her, he was all she had. So, gently and carefully, he put his arm around her and pulled her toward him. He did his best to keep it platonic and casual.

When he touched her, she stiffened at first, but he forced himself to keep his embrace featherlight. Within a moment the rigidity went out of her and she pressed her face into the hollow of his shoulder, her tears soaking into his shirt.

He said things. Later, he could never remember what, but whatever he'd whispered to her as her sobs faded, they must have helped because she stayed there, in the circle of his arms, for a long time. After a while he stopped talking and just sat and held her, torturing himself by mentally cataloging every wonderful, sexy thing about her. Her soft fragrant hair, her slender shoulder with the sweet curve that his fingers caressed, the warmth of her breath against his skin.

Finally, her breaths stopped hitching and became relatively quiet. A few moments later he felt her sigh, then she lifted her head and pulled away from him. He didn't try to hold on to her, but he did leave his arm draped around her shoulder. She let it stay there, too.

He looked at her with a little smile. "Better?"

She made a face. "I don't like to cry. It just messes up my face and gives me a headache."

He laughed softly and she did, too.

Then she nodded. "Yes. Better." She met his gaze and he marveled at how blue her eyes were. He'd thought from the beginning that they were lovely.

"I think you have the most beautiful eyes I've ever seen."

She blinked and her tongue slipped out to moisten her lips as her gaze slid downward from his eyes to his lips.

He had a sudden need to swallow—hard. Here they went again. Just like before, he sat perfectly still and hoped like hell that she didn't kiss him, because he was already very much on the edge. If she so much as leaned toward him, the tension and anticipation that now zinged through him would erupt into full-on lust, and he'd have to stop himself from jumping on her like a horny teenage boy.

She's your responsibility. Your responsibility.

"Look, Laney—" he said stupidly, because he had no idea what to say. He was just desperate to stop her from looking at his mouth. It worked. Her gaze snapped back to his face.

"Ethan?" she whispered. Her eyes were dewy

bright and her cheeks were pink. He brushed his thumb across her flushed skin and her head inclined toward his touch.

Laney saw the question in Ethan's eyes. She had no idea how to respond, wasn't even sure she was reading his expression correctly.

He leaned forward, his gaze moving from her eyes to her lips. Then, as she let her eyes drift shut, he brushed her mouth with his, nothing more than a featherlike touch, but the impact of it was stunning. For that brief second, she'd felt as though someone had lit her lips on fire.

His gaze flitted upward, toward her eyes, then back down and he inclined his head and kissed her again. This time, the touch of his mouth on her wasn't featherlike at all. His mouth was firm, his kiss demanding. Laney took a short gasping breath before he covered her mouth with his and kissed her more deeply.

She let her lips part. Her tongue met his. She

tasted him as he tasted her. She couldn't believe the rush of feelings his kiss was evoking in her. She felt it like a river of lava, flowing through her, igniting fires everywhere it went. And she wanted more. She moaned with the yearning.

Ethan went still. "Am I hurting your arm?" he whispered.

"No," she gasped. At this point, if it were burning like the fires of hell she wouldn't admit it. That's how badly she wanted to stay in his arms. That's how badly she wanted him to make love to her.

"Are you sure—?" he started.

She'd had enough of his caution. She leaned forward and kissed him openmouthed, teasing him with her tongue, daring him to kiss her back as intimately as she was kissing him.

He hesitated for an instant, but then with a throaty groan, he met her boldness with his own. He opened his mouth, kissing her fully, deeply, exploring with his tongue in a rhythmic dance with hers. His hand cupped her cheek and his thumb played that magic again across the apex of her lower lip, pulling her deeper into his spell.

Her arms slid up to wrap around his neck. The bruises on her arm ached, but the pain was nothing compared to the exquisite pleasure of his kiss.

After a long time, Ethan pulled away again. This time though, he left his hand on the bony curve of her shoulder. His gaze met hers, searching. She let her eyes drift shut and wet her lips with her tongue. He skimmed his fingertips across her sensitized skin, tracing a sensuous path across the sloping line of her collarbone and on to the small indentation below the column of her throat.

She swallowed and opened her eyes to meet the question in his. In answer, she caught his hand and guided it downward, downward, until his fingers nestled in the hollow between her breasts. He pulled her close and kissed her deeply, leaving her breathless. Then he planted light, erotic kisses along the line of her jaw.

She gasped as he moved upward to nibble on her earlobe, then back down to savor the soft, sensitive skin beneath her jaw. At the same time, he cupped her breast and played with her nipple until it was hard and throbbing.

"Ethan?" she panted.

He pushed her back against the couch cushions, fumbling at her waist. Desperate to feel him inside her, she brushed his hands away and undid her slacks so he could slide them down. Then he rose to his knees above her to undo his own clothes.

Once his arousal sprang free he sank between her knees and pressed it, smooth and hot and hard, against her. She whimpered in yearning. His hand slid between them and he touched her, tested her, caressed her. She felt the flowing warmth that signaled her readiness. He did, too—she knew because he made a sensual growling sound, deep in his throat, then lifted himself and pushed into her with a shuddering gasp.

Laney inhaled sharply as he sank into her, filling her with exquisite pleasure. Without hesitation she lifted herself to meet him and then both of them were frenzied, too turned on to be gentle or careful. They moved as one, not because they knew each other's bodies and preferences, but because they seemed fused together, feeding off each other's passion.

Within what seemed to be seconds, Laney's body tightened in almost unbearable anticipation. As Ethan thrust harder and deeper than he had so far, she felt herself explode into a thousand tiny shards.

Ethan came almost immediately after, with a soft, shuddering cry. The two of them collapsed against the couch cushions, panting. Soon their harsh breaths slowed and softened, and they lay together, languid and spent. Laney trailed her fingers across his shoulders, raising goose bumps where she touched. Ethan's hand rested against Laney's cheek, where his thumb played lightly back and forth, mimicking the flutter of butterfly wings.

When the doorbell rang, Ethan started and Laney stiffened beside him. They'd fallen asleep, still in each other's arms.

"Oh, no," Laney whispered, sitting up and squirming to pull her pants up and fasten them. "That better not be—" She pushed away from him and struggled to her feet, still fumbling with the button at her waist. She smoothed her hands down the front of the pants, then pushed her fingers through her hair to tame it a little.

She put her hands to her cheeks, then fanned them with her hands.

"Be who?" he asked as he stood and fastened his pants.

"Oh, nothing. A stupid girl with a silly cat!" she groused as she headed for the front door.

He followed her, grabbing the edges of his shirt and settling it on his shoulders. He wiped a hand across his face, trying to banish the haze of sleep. He had no idea who the stupid girl was or if she or her silly cat might be dangerous, but he wasn't taking any chances. His gun was in his car, damn it. So he stood behind Laney and to her left, prepared to jump the person if needed.

With her hand on the doorknob, Laney called out, "Who is it?" Her voice was after-sex husky and it sent a spear of lust through him. He shook his head and forced himself to concentrate on who might be on the other side of the door.

"My name's Emma. I'm selling candy for our marching band," a small, childish voice said.

Laney's breath whooshed out in a long sigh. She grabbed her purse and pulled out a five-dollar bill.

Ethan stopped her with a hand on her arm as she prepared to open the door. "Hang on. It's almost ten o'clock. Late for a child to be going door-to-door. Step back as you open it. If it's not just a child selling candy, I'll have a straight shot to jump them."

She frowned at him, but did as she was told.

Ethan stiffened as the door swung open, but it actually was a little girl standing on the stoop with a woman who was obviously her mother. The girl smiled shyly.

"What in the world are you doing out this

late?" Laney asked, eyeing the mother, who smiled sheepishly.

"She forgot to tell me about it," she said.

"And it's not late," the little girl said, sounding much older than her years. "I go to bed when Mommy and Daddy do. Do you want some candy?" She held up a cardboard carrier.

"Sure," Laney said. "How much will this buy?" she asked, proffering the bill.

The little girl grinned. "Two boxes. And you get a dollar back."

"Good," Laney replied, smiling. "Give me two boxes, and you keep the dollar for your marching band."

"Mommy! She said keep the dollar!"

"I know, Emma. I heard her." The mother mouthed *Thank you* as she led the little girl back down the sidewalk.

Laney closed the door.

"What stupid girl and silly cat?" Ethan asked

her as she put her purse back on the foyer table and walked back into the living room.

"Oh, it really was nothing," she answered, making a dismissive gesture. "Last night some annoying little housewife from down the street thought her cat had gotten under my car. She wanted me to come out and help her find it." Laney flexed her shoulder and winced.

"You didn't go out there, did you?" Ethan asked, a faint warning buzz taking hold at the edge of his brain.

"Yes. I thought it might save me from being talked to death." She shook her head. "I'm not even convinced there was a cat. I never saw it. We looked all around and underneath my car. Then finally she said she saw it running back toward her house. So she just headed off down the street with barely a thank you."

"And that's all that happened?"

"Yes," she said. "You know, if she'd waited

instead of bothering me, within ten minutes that cat would have been back at her door wanting food. Then, not five minutes later, little Miss Carolyn knocked on my door again. She had my phone! She said she'd picked it up off the ground near the driver's-side door and—get this—forgotten to tell me."

The buzz in his brain grew louder. "How long did it take you to look for the cat?" he asked.

"Maybe five or six minutes."

"And what time was it?"

"When I went outside? I don't know. Around seven or so? When she handed me my phone it was seven-ten."

"So it was dark." He didn't like the direction his brain was taking. Had the young woman gotten Laney outside and distracted her while an accomplice had snatched her phone from her purse? But why would anyone go to all that trouble to take her phone, then give it back to her? "And she wanted you on the far side of your car from the house?"

"Okay Detective Delancey," she said. "What's with the third degree?"

"Where's your phone now?"

"In my purse." She got it and handed it to him.

He examined it. There was only one explanation he could think of for lifting her phone and then bringing it back. "What's your password?"

"Hey," she said. "What are you doing?"

"Give me your password."

She did.

"Damn, Laney. That's the last four digits of your phone number. That's the default password for every phone out there. You're supposed to change it as soon as you get the phone."

Laney gave a small shrug of her right shoulder. "I know," she said. "Lazy."

"Yeah," he said in disgust. Then a moment later, "Not just lazy. Dangerous."

"Dangerous? Why?"

"Your phone's been bugged."

"My phone? Bugged?" Laney repeated Ethan's words. "As in, they can hear what we're saying? I thought a bugging device was—big. Too big to go inside a cell phone."

"This is a totally new technology. It's software-based bugging. They can track your whereabouts with GPS any time the phone is on. They can hack into your conferencing software with their number so their phone rings when you make or receive a call, and they can listen to all your telephone conversations. I've seen it before. Whenever your phone rings or you dial out, the software alerts them and they can record or listen in on your conversation."

She shivered. "I should have known. There was something about that girl. She looked vaguely familiar, but she also seemed a little too eager. Not so much worried about her cat as worried about getting me to help her. So someone walked right into my house, got my phone out of my purse, and I didn't even see them. Ethan, that really scares me."

"It should. Any other time it might have been just a rather annoying incident with a neighbor. But you're involved in a murder. Remember me telling you to be careful? To call me if *anything* unusual happened? The woman wanting you to come help her find her cat qualifies as unusual. You should have called me when it happened."

"I know. I know," Laney said, looking chagrined. "But why would anyone do that? What do they think I'm going to say on my phone that will help them?"

Ethan shook his head. "If it's the murderer, he may want to find out for sure how much you know, or if you recognized him. You said the girl looked familiar. Have you seen her around the neighborhood before? Walking? Driving? Calling her cat?"

Laney shook her head. "No. I'm gone all day and I don't know most of my neighbors. But when I say she looked vaguely familiar, it's not that I've seen her around. I'm not sure I can explain it. It was more like she reminded me of someone. Like you'll see someone who reminds you of an actor, but you can't place which actor it is. You know?"

Ethan nodded without looking up. He was staring at her phone. She'd handled it all day and he'd handled it just now. If there were any usable prints of the person who bugged it, it would be a miracle. But he was going to try it anyway. "Can you get me a paper bag? If you don't have one a plastic baggie will do."

"For what?" she asked. "Wait. Are you thinking you can get prints? I'm sorry, but I wiped the case with a wet cloth when she gave it to me. I cleaned the screen, too. I doubt there's anything left on it."

"I'd still like to try," he said.

While he waited for her to bring him the bag, he turned off her phone. When she held out a small paper bag, he slipped the phone into it, then stuck it into his pants pocket. "I'll take it to the crime lab first thing in the morning. See if they can lift a print off the surface or the keys. It's a long shot, since you cleaned it, but it's worth a try."

"And you'll have the bug taken out?" she asked hopefully.

He shook his head. "I don't think so. No. If we remove the bug, then they'll know we're on to them. But if I leave it bugged, you *have* to watch what you say. Remember, the man who murdered Senator Sills could be listening in." He pulled out his phone. "And when you're driving, I want you to turn the phone off. I don't want them tracking you by GPS. Now, I'm going to call a couple of officers to canvass the neighborhood to find your friend Carolyn. I have a feeling they won't have any luck."

"If she was just distracting me while her partner bugged my phone, do you think he bugged the house, too? Can they hear what we're saying now?"

"I doubt he had time to set a bug in here, but I'll have your house swept. We don't want to take any chances." He quickly made the call.

When he hung up, Laney said, "You're going to have all that done tonight? We won't get any sleep."

And as she predicted, it was after three o'clock in the morning before the last of the lab techs left. Laney felt as though she were sleepwalking. She'd made coffee for the techs but she hadn't drunk any herself, fearful that she wouldn't be able to sleep after they left if she filled up on caffeine.

When Ethan came back into the living room, Laney looked up at him with sleepy eyes. "So what did they find?"

"You want the full rundown? I told you once they finished with your room you could go to bed."

"No I couldn't. Not with my house being swept and scoped and whatever else, like a crime scene."

"Nothing was scoped," he said, smiling.

"Fine. Make fun of me. But wait until after I go to bed. Right now I want to know what they found."

"Okay. Your phone was clean of prints and the techs agreed with me that if they removed the bug or tampered with it in any way, it would alert whoever is on the other end. The computer guy did look at it for a few minutes, to see what he could find. He couldn't find anything he could trace. He said whoever bugged it was good. As far as your house, it's clean. No bugs."

"That's a relief," Laney said. "So what about Carolyn?"

"She doesn't live around here anywhere. My officers knocked on doors all over this subdivision, and the phone tech back at the precinct checked every address and phone number within a mile radius. No Carolyn."

"Wow," Laney said. "I should have had more sense than to play into her little charade. I should have called you. We'll probably never find out who she is."

"Well, I hope we do, because she and the person who walked into your house and bugged your phone are both working for the murderer."

Laney shivered and stood, ready to go to bed. But she thought of a question she should have asked hours ago. "Ethan? These people obviously know where I live. If they—if the murderer wanted to find me and—you know, kill me, he wouldn't have any trouble. So why the GPS and the bug?"

"Think about it. What happened this afternoon? That guy in the sports car knew where you were. He waited for you to come out of the storage lot and then he rammed you. He probably wanted whatever you were picking up from your storage building. Did you tell anybody on the phone that you were going by there?"

"No, I don't—oh, wait," she said. "When I talked to Senator Sills's secretary about the meetings this—well, yesterday morning, I told her I had to leave by four o'clock because I wanted to go by my storage building in Kenner before it got dark. Oh, I don't like this."

"So he figured you'd be getting something from your storage building that pertained to the case. But now they probably know that I've got it, since you had that truck driver call me to tell me about your accident."

"But if I turn the phone off when I'm driving, they can't track me, and if I don't say anything on the phone, they won't know where I'm going."

"That's the plan."

ETHAN TURNED OVER for about the thirtieth time and tried his best to stay asleep. But this time there was more going on than just being disgustingly uncomfortable. His phone was ringing. He sat up, trying to remember exactly where he was and why he'd slept on a lumpy couch. Squinting, he peered around him. This wasn't his place. It was Laney's house. He was sleeping, or trying to, on her lumpy couch. The night before and Laney came back to him in a flash. Odd that it hadn't felt lumpy when they were both on it. Although, as intense and sexy as their coupling had been, he doubted he'd have noticed a tsunami.

When he stood and looked at himself, he remembered that he'd taken off his pants, knowing that he was going to have to wear them again today. They were draped over the opposite side of the couch. He leaned forward to grab them.

"Is that your phone or mine? You have both of them." It was Laney, standing in the foyer doorway with a sheet wrapped around her. She held the two edges together with a hand at her chest.

Ethan grabbed his pants and held them in front of him as he turned around. It occurred to him that for all their intimacy of the night before, they hadn't yet seen each other naked.

And now they were standing in front of each other as if they'd never seen each other before at all. "Yeah. Sorry if it woke you."

It rang again at that instant and he groped in his pockets until he found it. It was Dixon. "Hey, Dix. What's up? You're calling awfully early."

"Not that early," Dixon answered. "It's after eight. What are you doing? I ran by your house last night and you weren't there."

"That's right. I'm at Laney's."

"I got your message about Laney's accident, the phone bug and everything, but you didn't mention you were planning to stay there all night. What the hell are you up to?"

Ethan clenched his jaw. "What did you call about, Dixon?" he grated. He saw Laney turn and head back down the hall.

"I got corralled about Laney's accident as soon as I walked in the door this morning.

Seems a Detective Benoit of the Kenner Police Department thought you'd have sent him the official request you promised first thing this morning. He said it's for some evidence that was found in Ms. Montgomery's car."

"Well, I considered first thing to be more like nine o'clock than eight. They get 'em up early over in Kenner, don't they?" Ethan said. He heard the water come on in the bathroom. "I'll get that request sent as soon as I get in. We should be there at the station no later than nine. Depends on how long it takes Laney to get dressed."

"Delancey?" Dixon snapped. "I hope you've got better sense than to do what I'm really afraid you've already done."

Ethan was not going to answer that. "That accident was no accident, Dixon. She stopped at the storage facility to pick up her dad's financial records, which, by the way, you'll be seeing today, because her dad withdrew large sums of money every week for the past ten years."

"Ten years?" Dixon's voice grew excited.

"Yeah. How long do you think it'll take to get those withdrawals matched with Sills's deposits?"

"If they match."

"Yeah, right. If they match. But they're going to match, I'll guarantee it."

"Yeah, okay. But even if they do match, what have we got? Obviously Montgomery didn't kill Sills." Dixon sighed. "I'll let you know what I find out. The reason I called was to tell you that we have Sills's safe-deposit box. So if you can tear yourself away from Ms. Montgomery, why don't you come on over to the courthouse and I'll show you some interesting stuff."

"I won't have any problem *tearing myself away* from Laney, Dixon. So get that superior smirk off your face right now. I can't see it but I know it's there." Ethan heard a noise and turned to see Laney standing in the living room doorway, dressed. The hurt look on her face told him she'd heard what he'd said about tearing himself away from her. He held up a finger to signal to her that he'd be just another minute.

She turned and went into the kitchen without acknowledging that she'd noticed him at all, much less seen his signal.

"We'll be there within half an hour, okay?" he said, the irritation obvious in his voice. "I'll see you then." He hung up. "Laney?" he called. "How're you feeling this morning?"

She stepped out of the kitchen into the foyer. "I'm fine," she said coolly. "So don't worry for a second about having to tear yourself away from me. I can take care of myself."

Ethan scowled at her. "Look, Dixon was kidding me, giving me a hard time for staying over here last night. I was repeating what he'd said, that's all. Don't take offense to something I say to my partner. Most of our conversations are a mixture of ribbing and a sort of shorthand that we use to communicate when we're at a crime scene or tracking a perp."

She shrugged. "Thanks for the explanation. Are you taking my phone in this morning? When can I get it back?"

"You can get it back now. One of the lab techs examined it and took prints last night. I cleaned it and left it on the table near the front door."

She retrieved the phone from the table and started back toward the kitchen. "What time are you leaving?"

"I'm not leaving—*we're* leaving," he answered sharply. "Haven't you been listening to me?"

"No, I'd rather not go to the station with you.

I'd rather stay here, in my own house, where I'm perfectly safe. You can call me and let me know which dealership has my car. I'll get in touch with them and have them bring me a loaner. Then I can be out of your hair completely."

"Okay, that does it. You're coming with me. There's no way I'm leaving you here alone. I've already explained to you several times that you could be in danger. After yesterday, I'm certain you *are* in danger. Now, Dixon has Sills's safe-deposit box. I want to find out what's in it. Don't you?"

"You mean I can see it?"

"No, you can't see it. But you can wait at the station and when I find out what's inside it I'll let you know."

"I can wait here," she said stubbornly.

"I suppose you could, but you won't," he replied, just as stonily, "because I'm not letting you out of my sight."

THE NEXT DAY Dixon knocked on the door of the small shotgun house on Perrier Street while Ethan stood aside. When the door opened, Dixon smiled. "Hey, Boone," he said.

Detective Boone Carter had been near retirement when Dixon had caught his first homicide—the purported murder of Ethan's cousin, Rosemary Delancey, who was now Dixon's wife. Ethan had never met Detective Carter, but he'd heard a lot about him. The detective had been a legend on the streets of the French Quarter back in the day.

"Hey, Lloyd. Man, you still look wet behind the ears to me. How long has it been?" Boone held the screen door open for them.

"Boone, this is my partner, Ethan Delancey," Dixon said, once they were inside.

Ethan held out his hand and Boone took it. "Yep. You definitely look familiar. Your granddaddy was Con Delancey, wasn't he?"

"Yes, sir."

"Con Delancey," Carter said again, shaking his head. "I'll be a monkey's uncle! You look a lot like him, son. He was a son of a bitch, but he was a grand man."

"Yes, sir. Thank you, sir," Ethan said.

Boone gestured toward the back of the house. Ethan followed Dixon through the small house that had gotten its name because a person could stand on the front porch and shoot a shotgun through the front door and hit nothing but air, if all the doors were open.

"Go on, go on. Out the back door," Boone said. "You'll see what I been spending my time on since I've been retired."

They stepped out the back door onto a concrete patio with a stone fountain square in the middle of it. The fountain was about the size of the kitchen they'd just walked through, and the bowl of the fountain held several koi. Surrounding the fountain and the patio were assorted ferns and other tropical plants.

"This is beautiful," Dixon said.

Ethan whistled. It was beautiful. It looked like a tropical hideaway on a luxurious island. The plants hid the small patio from view of the neighbors, and by the same token they hid the wire fences and peeling paint of the neighboring houses from anyone sitting on the patio.

"Sit down, sit down. Maggie made some iced tea. Help yourself."

Ethan poured himself a glass from the pitcher full of ice and tea and Dixon did the same. Boone already had a glass sitting beside his chair.

He took a swig, then looked at the two of them. "So what's up at the Eighth? 'Cause I know you didn't come here to admire the view."

"It is spectacular," Dixon said, propping an

ankle on the other knee and taking a long swallow of tea.

Ethan knew that it was his job to question
Boone about the incident they'd uncovered in
Darby Sills's safe-deposit box. They'd found a
copy of the domestic disturbance report Boone
Carter had written that had apparently never
been filed, because despite Farrantino's metic-
ulous search of the case files for the past ten
years, there was no mention of an incident involving Darby Sills.

Ethan sat forward. "Detective Carter?"

"Boone, son. Call me Boone."

"Boone," Ethan said reluctantly. He didn't
feel right calling the gray-haired man by his
first name. He'd heard stories about Carter's
years as a detective. To him the man sounded
like a superhero; and now that he'd met him,
he looked like one, too. Still in great shape,
Carter had a loose, predatory confidence that

Ethan was sure had intimidated even the most hardened of criminals.

"So tell me what you got to tell me son, and I'll see if I can help you guys out at all."

"You know that Darby Sills was murdered four days ago," Ethan started, but was interrupted by Carter's booming laugh.

"Yep," the detective said, grinning. "I knew it. I know exactly why you two are here." He sat forward and rested his elbows on his knees. "Hit me with it."

"Well, sir. Among the contents of Senator Sills's safe-deposit box was a police domestic disturbance report made out by you of an incident with Sills and a prostitute."

Carter was staring down at the patio floor. He nodded. "That's right," he said.

Ethan waited, but Carter didn't say anything else. He looked at Dixon, who just raised his eyebrows and took another swallow of iced tea. So Ethan waited, too, sipping at the too-sweet tea.

"When I heard somebody had shot Darby, I wondered if it had all finally come to a head." Carter shook his head without looking up. "What an idiot."

Ethan frowned. "Who?" he asked.

Carter sat up and picked up his glass. "Darby, of course. He had a lot of problems—couldn't keep it in his pants, couldn't pass up a free meal, no matter who was buying or what kind of strings were attached, and worst of all, couldn't stand to throw anything away." Carter chuckled. "I'll bet y'all found every receipt for everything he ever bought, including gum."

At that, Dixon let out a laugh. "You're right about that. And I've had the pleasure of going through all that."

"So," Carter drawled. "See anything in that safe-deposit box about Buddy Davis?"

"Buddy Davis? Why?"

Carter sent him a wry look. "Just making conversation."

"Detective—sorry, Boone," Ethan said, "is there something you know about Davis that might help us with the investigation of Sills's murder?"

Carter stood and walked over to the fountain. From the wide ledge surrounding the pool, he picked up a small container and sprinkled some food into the water. "Let's see, I guess it's been ten years ago now. What was that girl's name? Oh, I remember. Cristal Waters. She pronounced it with the emphasis on the *AL.* Made sure I spelled it right on the police report. *Like the champagne,* she told me."

Ethan watched him sprinkle a few more

grains of fish food, then stand and watch them crowd one another as they fought for the morsels. "I was called to a real skanky house, way over across Rampart. Man, I couldn't believe my eyes. First thing I saw was Darby Sills, hopping on one foot and crashing into walls, trying to get his pants on. Cristal was holding a wet washcloth against her lip, which was split so bad the cloth was red with blood. Her eye was swollen, too, and starting to turn purple. When she saw me, she started yelling. I swear I think it took me a full minute to figure out what she was saying. She was yelling Buddy Davis's and Elliott Montgomery's names at the top of her lungs."

"Montgomery?" Ethan said, a queasy dread suddenly pressing on his chest. "Are you sure she said Elliott Montgomery?"

Carter stopped laughing and scowled at Ethan. "Yeah," he drawled. "I am."

"What was she saying about them?"

"Well what do you think, sonny boy? She swore they were there with Darby."

Ethan winced. This was bad. Laney had been devastated by the thought that her dad was being blackmailed. She would be crushed when she found out that it was because of a prostitute. "Did you find any evidence that either of them had been there? Because there's nothing in the report."

"Do you think it mattered one damn bit whether there was evidence or not? Why do you think that report was never filed?"

Ethan shook his head.

"Because about five minutes after I called in to dispatch that I was answering a domestic dispute call and gave the address, and about two minutes after I walked into that room and saw what I saw and heard what I heard, I got a phone call from the commander, telling me to get Sills out of there and make sure nothing was ever heard about the incident again."

"Who was your commander?" Ethan asked, but Carter was still talking.

"And don't think for a minute that it was the Eighth Precinct commander's decision. That order came straight from the superintendent."

"Because it was Senator Sills," Ethan said.

"That's right."

"But what about the girl? What happened to her?"

"She never changed her story that those two were there with Sills," Carter said. "Even though she swore that Sills was the only one who'd touched her. But somebody paid her to keep quiet. I don't know if it was Sills or Davis or Montgomery or—even the department."

Could some or all of the money that Laney's dad withdrew have gone to Cristal Waters?

It was possible, but Ethan didn't think so. As much as it galled him to think that someone in the highest ranks of the NOPD would pay off a witness to protect a prominent politician, that seemed like the most believable explanation. Second most believable—Sills. Maybe Sills extorted money from Davis and Montgomery to pay Cristal.

Carter laughed. "It would have been a great story, wouldn't it? Those three, the prominent statesman, the famous televangelist and the important lobbyist, all caught with their pants down—literally and figuratively." He turned to the fountain, picked up his box of fish food and closed it, then sat back down and picked up his nearly empty glass of tea. "So you guys think Buddy Davis killed Darby Sills?"

Chapter Nine

By the time Ethan and Dixon returned to the police station, Laney felt as if she were going out of her mind. She knew they'd gone to talk to retired Detective Boone Carter about a police report they'd found in Senator Sills's safe-deposit box. The report had never been officially filed.

It was less than three hours after Ethan had told her he was not going to let her out of his sight and here she was, back in an empty interview room waiting by herself.

She picked up the coffee cup she'd been given

by an officer an hour ago. It was stone-cold, of course, and just as muddy tasting as it had been when it was hot. With a grimace of distaste, she set it back down and stood up. The room was small and most of it was taken up by the table and chairs. She walked over to the barred window and looked out at Royal Street.

Last night had been a stunning night, in many senses of the word. The idea that her father really had been paying blackmail to Darby Sills had ripped away the last vestige of illusion she'd had about him. Like most little girls, she had worshiped her father, maybe more than most, since her mother had died when she was eleven and so for most of her life it had just been her and him.

She supposed most children eventually found out that their parents were not superheroes, that they were just people who made mistakes and did things they regretted. She wondered if she was later than most learning that painful lesson.

She knew Ethan thought she was naive. She'd seen it in his eyes. He'd had a hard time believing she'd never wondered about the money her father had in his savings account, or the type of work he did or why he received such generous bonuses. She wished she could explain to Ethan that she'd never known another child whose parent had done the same kind of work her dad had. She'd never had anyone to compare him with.

Thinking of Ethan brought back the memory of the night before and their frenzied lovemaking. It had started innocently enough. She'd been upset, not so much that her father was being blackmailed, but that he'd done something to make himself vulnerable to blackmail. She didn't like to cry, and she'd have given almost anything not to have broken down in front of Ethan, but he'd surprised her. He'd been as tender and solicitous as he'd been that first night in the E.R. So when he'd reached out to comfort her, she'd eased right into his arms. It had felt right somehow, to let him hold her and whisper to her.

Then, when the tender comfort had changed to desire, she'd been as frenzied as he. They'd torn at each other's clothes, coming together with a passion she'd never felt before. Ethan was harsh and demanding and yet at the same time careful. She herself had quickly abandoned all care. For her, nothing had mattered except being as close, as intimate with him as was humanly possible. Their climaxes had been explosive and nearly simultaneous.

For those moments he was not a police detective and she was not a crime victim. There was no murder, no blackmail. The world had dissolved and the two of them may as well have been transformed into pure desire.

But this morning, their fiery lovemaking and their tender aftermath might have been just a dream. In the harsh light of day it seemed insane to think for even one second that they could be anything other than two strangers brought together by the insanity of a violent crime. His job was to solve the murder of Senator Darby Sills and her job—her job was to answer his questions and do her best to identify the faceless black-clad person who had killed the senator.

Once the case was solved, she doubted she'd ever see Detective Ethan Delancey again. As she tried to suppress that depressing thought, her phone rang. When she checked the display, the number was unknown. She grimaced. She was not in the mood for more questions about what she'd seen or requests for interviews. But here she was, stuck at the police station, with nothing to do, not even a magazine to read, so, knowing she was probably going to regret it, she answered the phone.

To her delight, it was the dealership where her car had been towed. With a grateful sigh she gave them her personal and billing information and asked them how long it would take before her car would be ready.

"It's going to be a few days, ma'am," the woman told her. "Would you like for us to arrange a loaner car? You do have that option with your insurance."

She opened her mouth to say yes, but Ethan's concern about her being in danger echoed in her head. "I'm not sure yet," she said. "Can I call back when I decide?"

The woman assured her she could, and told her she'd call her when her car was fixed and ready for pickup.

Laney hung up and called voice mail to listen to her messages. Most of them were the same, but there was a message from Senator Sills's secretary, letting her know that the funeral would be on Sunday, two days away. She saved the message as a reminder and put her phone away.

She'd just about decided to march out into the squad room and ask somebody where she could get a cold drink, and by the way just how long did it take to drive to somebody's house, interview them and drive back to the police station, when the door opened and Ethan came in, his phone caught precariously between his shoulder and chin as he scribbled on a small pad.

"What did you find out?" she whispered, but he ignored her.

"Right," he said. "It's not Waters? Mackey, okay. Phone number?" He glanced at Laney but his expression didn't change.

Laney could hear the female voice on the other end of the phone. She didn't know what they were talking about, but she listened.

"Is there an address?" He set the pad down on the table and took the phone in his left hand, holding it a little closer to his ear. Then he sat. "Can you spell that, please?"

She could still hear the woman but her voice was much more muffled. What she heard sounded like "Burgin." She looked down at the pad where Ethan was writing. He printed, in almost block letters. Looking upside down at the pad, Laney read what Ethan had written: "8830 Bourgin—Meraux." She had an address and either a first name or a last name. *Mackey.*

Suddenly Ethan glanced up at her. She lowered her gaze to her fingernails and picked at a speck on one. Apparently it wasn't enough to fool him because he picked up his pad and stood. "No," he said, in answer to a question

Laney hadn't heard. "Hold on." He stepped over to the door and opened it and went through. As the door was closing, Laney heard him say. "Okay. No, the name I have is Cristal, with an I. A prostitute that Sills—"

The door closed, muffling the rest of what he said.

Laney immediately grabbed her purse, digging in it for her phone. She didn't want to miss anything that Ethan said, but she didn't want to forget what she'd already heard either. She turned her phone on and waited impatiently as it booted up. Then she accessed her address book and pressed a button to enter a new contact. Quickly she keyed in Cristal Mackey, 8830 Bourgin Street, Meraux, Louisiana, and clicked Save. While she was writing her brain was racing. "A prostitute that Sills" was what Ethan had said.

A prostitute that Sills had what? Shared with

her father maybe? She shuddered, stopping that thought right there. She couldn't even entertain the idea of her father being involved with a prostitute. But what else could have forced her father to pay Sills blackmail? Nothing that she could even imagine. And now, because of all this, she was imagining all sorts of illegal or immoral activities. How much more damage could she endure to the memory of the man who'd born her and reared her for most of her life?

She held her breath and listened for Ethan's voice. It sounded as though he was still talking to the woman. She accessed the web feature and started to type in the woman's name, but at that instant, Ethan's muffled voice changed timbre. Was he saying goodbye?

She stuck the phone under her chair just as he stepped back inside the room, pocketing his phone.

"Well?" she said, leaning forward. "What did you find out from the detective?"

"A lot of stuff," Ethan answered evasively. "And right now we can't even follow up on it, because there's a big press conference in an hour and a half. Commander Wharton says Superintendent Fortenberry feels he needs to update the media about the progress we're making on the Sills case. He wants Dixon and me to help with the prep ahead of time and to be visible on the podium while he addresses the media."

"And you're going to leave me stuck here all that time?" She shook her head. "No. I want to go home. I want to get into my pajamas and get into my bed and sleep for about twenty-four hours. Please."

"Nope. There's no way you're going back to your house by yourself. Are you not convinced yet that whoever killed Sills knows who you are and where you live? We talked about this. These people are watching you, tracking you, listening to you. When are you going to figure out just how much danger you're in?"

"Okay," she said, trying to keep her voice steady, "I won't go home. I'll get a hotel room. It won't be as good as my own bed, but at least I'll be able to sleep."

Ethan was already shaking his head. "We already know what can happen in a hotel room."

"Oh, come on," she said tiredly. "How good do you think this person is? Are you telling me the only way I can be safe is if you force me to sit here in the middle of dozens of police officers? Well, I'm pretty sure I still have rights. Do I have to go through this again? Detective Delancey, am I under arrest?"

He glared at her. "Don't start with me, Laney—"

"Am I?" She gave him glare for glare. "Because unless you have something to charge me with, I don't think you can keep me here against my will."

"How about resisting arrest?"

Laney was so angry her ears burned. "How about I tell them—" She stopped. There was no way she could betray him by telling anyone about their night together. She knew he regretted it. She knew enough to know he'd be on very thin ice if anyone found out that he'd slept with a victim and a witness in his case, even if he protested that she was a more-than-willing partner. Even if *she* swore she'd been willing.

She knew she could not do that to him, and she was horrified at herself for even hinting that she might. "Ethan—" she started, wanting more than anything she'd ever wanted in her life to take back those few words.

But Ethan was staring at her, his expression carefully neutral. She hadn't stopped herself soon enough. He knew what she'd been about to say. "Okay," he said without inflection. "You can go home. I'll call my cousin Dawson and see if he has someone who can watch your house."

"Ethan, I didn't—I would never—"

He sliced his hand through the air in a dismissive gesture, refusing to let her apologize. "The name of the agency is D&D Security. An agent will park near your house and watch it. If anyone approaches, he'll get pictures, description and vehicle license plates. If the person acts in any way suspicious, he'll bring him in. He'll be there to protect you if anything happens."

"Ethan, I swear to you I would never ever betray you. Please don't do this. Don't assign me to a *babysitter*. That's just plain insulting." She had a plan forming in her head and a *babysitter* by any name had no part in it. "Not to mention ridiculous. There's no way that's happening. Besides, it'll cost a fortune. I can't afford it."

Ethan shrugged. "I can."

"I'm going home. If you want to hire somebody, fine. But they will not—" she pointed her finger at Ethan in emphasis "—will *not* tell me what I can and can't do and where I can and can't go. If you stick somebody out there to watch me, they'd better be good, because they just might have to keep up with me."

The muscle in Ethan's jaw ticked as he tried to maintain control. He was angrier than she'd ever seen him. While she wasn't actually afraid of him, he was pretty darn intimidating.

"Don't push me, Laney," he said.

She lifted her chin. Fine. She was angry, too. "Don't push *me*."

"I don't have time to worry about you. You've got two choices. I *will* put you in lockup for your own protection or I'll hire an agent to watch your house *while you* stay in it."

She didn't speak.

"It's your choice," he said.

"My house," she finally answered grudgingly.

"Good answer. When I get off work, I'll pick you up *at your house,* dismiss the agent and take you to my apartment."

"To your apartment? For what?" she demanded.

He stepped closer and looked down at her, his eyes blazing with anger. But that wasn't all she saw in their depths. She saw the same fire she'd seen last night as they came together. It was a fire so hot and yet so compelling that she was at once fearful of being burned and compelled to move toward it. For a moment, standing there in the interview room of the police station where anyone could be watching them through the two-way mirror, she felt an echo of the thrill of his hot flesh against hers and the overwhelming need to pull him to her and feel it all again.

He gave a small shake of his head and an irritating smirk curled his lip. "For your protection," he said with silky control. "What else?"

Laney blew out a harsh breath laced with frustration and embarrassment. He'd drawn her in, then deliberately rejected her. It was like a slap to the face. She stepped backward. "You are a—"

"Watch out, Ms. Montgomery," he drawled. "Anything you say can and will be used against you in a court of law."

She clamped her mouth shut and folded her arms, refusing to look at him. "May I get a ride to my house?" she asked icily.

"Yes, ma'am," he said. "I'll have one of the officers take you, and trust me, I intend to have your *babysitter* waiting for you by the time you get there."

As he opened the door and stepped back to let her exit before him, she remembered her phone on the floor underneath her chair. It occurred to her that it might be a good thing that she didn't have it with her, especially if she was going to carry out the plan that was blossoming in her brain. Without it, nobody could trace where she went using GPS. She tried to ignore the small voice that reminded her that without her phone, she couldn't call anyone if she got in trouble.

As soon as the officer who dropped her off at her house drove away, Laney examined her street and saw no cars parked at the curb. The ones that were in the driveways were either ones she recognized or didn't appear to have anyone inside them. Breathing a sigh of relief, she quickly walked across the street to her neighbors' and used their phone to call the car dealership.

"I would like a loaner car," she told the woman she'd talked to before. "I can take a cab if you don't have anyone to bring the car to me."

"As it happens, the van is picking up a customer who lives out your way, so I can send a driver with your car and the van can pick him up and bring him back."

Laney thanked her neighbor, then ran back to her house and changed into jeans and a hoodie, figuring it was more appropriate attire to go visiting on questionable streets in Meraux than her business pantsuit. She hoped she'd understood the snatches of Ethan's telephone conversation correctly, and that 8830 Bourgin Street in Meraux was where Cristal, the prostitute, lived. She had no idea what the woman had to do with Senator Sills's murder, but she was pretty sure what she'd done with Sills himself. For the entire time she'd worked for Senator Sills, she'd heard rumors that he liked to pay for sex. According to gossip, his penchant for prostitutes was what had finally broken up his marriage.

She glanced at the couch and the pillows, which had matching indentations. The memories of the night before and she and Ethan making love came back to her in a rush. Closing her eyes, she shook her head, but that did nothing to stop the thrill inside her as her brain fed her explicit images of why she'd had trouble sleeping the night before. If things were different, she'd lie down on the couch and lose herself in a daydream of the exquisite sensations he'd coaxed from her with his mouth and his body. Thinking of him, her body trembled in a tiny aftershock of her climax. She opened her eyes and saw the sheet and pillow piled on the coffee table, and the beautiful daydream dissolved.

Once she'd closed the front door on the girl and her mother selling candy, she'd turned to Ethan, thinking that he'd take her into his arms again. But that didn't happen. He'd bombarded her with questions about Carolyn and the cat, then he'd called in crime scene people and lab techs and had them go over her house with a fine-tooth comb.

When the forensic team finally left, he'd asked for a pillow so he could sleep on the couch. So much for beautiful, sexy daydreams. There was no time for them anyhow. If she was going to get out of here before her babysitter showed up and make it to Bourgin Street to talk to Cristal before the police got there, she needed to get a move on.

Just as she finished tying her running shoes, her doorbell rang. An arrow of fear struck the center of her chest. Who was it? Stepping over to the window, she peered through the blinds. It was a sedan with dealership tags. Thank goodness.

She opened the door to a man in a light blue shirt with his name on the pocket. He had a piece of paper in his hands. "Ma'am," he said. "Are you Elaine Montgomery? I'll need to see your driver's license please."

She showed him her license.

"Here's your key, and here's the insurance approval for you to get a loaner car. Keep that in the car, if you would. That serves as our insurance information in case of an accident."

She thanked him and grabbed her purse. As she headed toward the car, the driver walked down to the corner to wait for the courtesy van. She started the car and pulled to the intersection, feeling as though a monster were breathing down her neck—Ethan's babysitter.

At the corner, she spotted a large, dark-colored car several blocks down. Was that him? In the other direction, the courtesy van was braking as it pulled up to the corner.

Hurry, she silently told the van. She didn't want the driver around to tell the babysitter which way she'd gone.

It took her about twenty minutes to get to Meraux and follow the GPS in the loaner car to Bourgin Street. She drove down the street, but the loaner car's GPS didn't find 8830. So she parked on a side street and started walking. Getting away from her house without getting caught by the D&D agent was pretty much the extent of her plan, but she figured she could ask about Cristal Mackey at any little shops nearby or give her name to neighbors who might be sitting outside. Somebody was bound to know her, if she had understood the woman's real name correctly.

There weren't many people on the street, and those who were out looked rough. There were young men, boys really, who probably should have been in school but who were dressed to impress in ultrabaggy or ultraskinny jeans, appropriately sized T-shirts to match the jeans and either hoodies or colors. They loitered at corners or lounged on steps, smoking cigarettes and drinking beer out of bottles wrapped in brown paper bags.

An older woman was sweeping the stoop of her house, muttering to herself in what Laney thought was Spanish but couldn't be sure. When Laney walked past, the woman looked up and glared at her, bitter hatred in her black eyes.

She tried not to hurry, tried to look cool and nonchalant as she headed on down the street. Most of the buildings were old and peeling. Residences were mixed with shops and abandoned buildings. She passed a sign that advertised apartments to rent. She started to go inside, but on the door was a handwritten sheet of paper that read "Closed."

Sighing, she kept on down the street. Then she saw a narrow house that was painted green and had a few pansies in the front yard. She didn't see a sign with a street number, but it was on the 8800 block and for some reason it just felt like the right house.

She walked up the sidewalk to the three steps that led up to the door of the house. She rang an old, ornate brass doorbell and heard its deep ring inside the house. For a long time she heard nothing except the echo of the bell. There was no other sound, not even any change in the air that might hint that there was someone on the other side of the door.

After at least a minute a pleasant female voice called, "Who's there?"

"Ms. Mackey? My name is Elaine Montgomery," Laney said. "I'd like to talk to you about my father."

"What? Sorry. I don't know him."

"Please. He was Elliott Montgomery. I just have some questions about him."

"Nope. Don't know him."

Laney stepped closer to the door. "Ms. Mackey," she said as softly as she could and still have any expectation of being heard. "I'm alone. I don't want anything from you except to know more about my dad. Please."

There was a long pause, then, "You're alone?"

"Yes," Laney answered. "I promise you."

Another pause, this time so long that Laney almost gave up. But finally, she heard locks being undone. Then the door opened with the chain still on. The face that peered through the crack in the door was very attractive. Her eyes were a startling chartreuse color. She looked at Laney, then glanced around the hall behind her.

When she closed the door, for a split second Laney was afraid once again that she'd decided not to answer, but then the chain clanked and the door opened.

The woman was probably in her early to mid-forties, dressed in a pink pajama set with a flowered robe thrown on over it. Her blond hair was twisted up on the back of her head and fastened loosely with a barrette. She studied Laney for a few seconds, then nodded.

"Come in. I'm Cristy." She stepped back to let Laney in and for the first time, Laney saw the handgun she held.

"Oh, I—" Laney said, stopping and holding up her hands.

"Sorry," Cristy said, pointing the weapon at the floor and clicking on the safety. "Protection," she said wryly as she walked around the island that separated the living area from the kitchen and put the gun in a drawer.

The inside of the house was bright and airy. Tall casement windows sparkled behind billowy white sheer curtains. Next to the door was a table that held a telephone and a tall hammered copper vase with a narrow neck. As Laney looked around, she realized, as small as the house was, that everything she saw could have been in a special *tiny house* issue of *Architectural Digest.* "Your house is beautiful," she said.

"Thanks," Cristy said, her face brightening into a smile. "I can certainly see that you're El's daughter. "He talked about you all the time."

TWENTY-FIVE MINUTES later, Laney knew a lot more about her dad than she'd ever known before, maybe more than she'd ever wanted to know. But where she'd only pieced together a blurry snapshot of the man who had done something that he'd thought was worth over half a million dollars to hide, Cristy painted her a life-size portrait. Laney heard about a man who had suffered along with the wife he'd loved as she sank deeper and deeper into alcohol addiction and depression, until she'd finally destroyed her looks, her body and finally her life. A man who had taken on the task of raising a daughter alone, and who had fallen in love with a prostitute.

Christine Mackey, who had taken back her given name after twenty-plus years as Cristal Waters, looked at her watch and said that she had to get ready for work.

"I apologize," Laney said quickly. "I didn't intend to stay this long. But I can't tell you how much I appreciate you talking to me."

"I actually enjoyed it. Ever since I saw that Darby Sills was murdered I've been sitting on pins and needles, wondering when the police were going to show up at my doorstep. I knew that eventually getting that domestic disturbance call covered up would come back to bite him. I figured it would get me in trouble, too. But truthfully, I never saw them after that night."

"Them? You mean Senator Sills and my dad?"

"No. I mean Darby or Buddy Davis."

"Buddy Davis?" Laney was surprised, although she shouldn't have been. From the very beginning, there had been plenty of indication that Davis was right in the middle of all this.

"You know—" Cristy said, snapping her fingers. "I've got a picture."

Laney's heart skipped a beat. "A picture?"

Cristy smiled like the cat with canary feathers spilling from her mouth as she reached under her bed and pulled out a box full of photos. "I have no idea why Darby decided to bring Davis and Elliot with him that night. That was the first time I'd ever met your dad or Davis. But they were celebrating something and Darby had two bottles of Dewar's scotch. So after about an hour we were all getting drunk, except your dad. When Darby tried to make him drink more, El joked that he was the designated driver. So I pulled out my camera, which I always did when I had a new client. It was my own personal form of insurance."

"You got a picture of all three of them?" Laney heard the apprehension in her voice. Was there a picture of her father and the other two men *with* Cristal? She wasn't sure she could bear that.

"Honey, no. I didn't mean to worry you. It's not that kind of picture. I took one of the three of them laughing at some joke while Darby poured more scotch. Then El took one of myself and Darby and Buddy Davis. When it got to be ten o'clock, El said he had to get home because you were going to call.

"That made Darby angry. So he drank some more, and Buddy kept up with him. Buddy started asking me to do things for him and that just added fuel to Darby's fire. Then apparently, it dawned on him that I'd taken the pictures. He demanded the camera and when I wouldn't give it to him, he hit me. He got really violent. As soon as Darby started swinging, Buddy ran like a yellow dog with its tail between its legs and I called the police. By the time they got there, Darby had broken my jaw and was claiming I'd stolen money from him. I was terrified that they'd arrest me, so I threw out all the names I could think of, including your father's." She shook her head slightly. "That, by the way, is when I got the gun. And soon after that, thanks to your father, I quit the business and started working on getting a college degree."

While she'd talked, Cristy had been sorting through the pictures. "You won't believe some of the people whose photos are in this box. Here are the ones I was looking for," she said, holding up two small snapshots, then handing them to Laney.

Laney studied the first photo. It was odd to see her dad laughing and holding a glass up in a salute to a younger Sills and Davis. She looked at the second picture. In it, a truly beautiful Cristy, dressed in a glamorous negligee, stood between Sills and Davis. They were looking at her and she was smiling at the camera. The look on her face made Laney uneasy. She held the picture to the light and studied Cristy's face more closely. "You liked my dad," she said. It was a statement, not a question.

Cristy smiled wistfully. "Your dad was a

special man. I know that Darby was blackmailing him."

"You do?"

"El told me. I begged him to go to the police and expose Darby for what he really was, but he wouldn't. He wasn't paying blackmail to Darby for his own sake."

Laney knew what Cristy was about to say. Tears stung her eyes.

"He did it to protect me. He paid Darby and he sent money to me. I never wanted to take it but your father was pretty persuasive when he wanted to be."

"Thank you," Laney said, her heart aching with love and grief. "Thank you so much for telling me that. I couldn't understand why he would let anyone blackmail him. I couldn't believe he'd done something so awful he'd pay blackmail rather than admit it. But he was paying the senator to protect you. Oh, Cristy, you've given my dad back to me." She paused. "Did my dad love you, too?"

Cristy played with the sash of her robe. "He did. But I was Cristal Waters and your dad was Elliott Montgomery," she said with flat finality. "Now I really have to get dressed. I don't want to be late for work. I do counseling at a women's shelter on the evening shift."

Laney started to leave, then turned back at the door. "I don't have my phone with me. Do you have a smartphone? I'd like to photograph those two pictures and send them to my phone, just in case."

"I have a smartphone, but I have no idea how to send pictures. All I use it for is making calls," Cristy said, handing over her phone to Laney. "Send them to yourself. But Laney, I've worked very hard to leave Cristal Waters behind. Please keep my name out of it."

"It might be too late for that. The police know

your real name and your address. I got them when I eavesdropped on a detective," Laney said as she snapped a couple of shots of the two photos, then she deleted the photos and the sent files from Cristy's phone.

"Great," Cristy said. "So I was right to be on pins and needles. They'll probably be here any minute now."

"Cristy, call Detective Ethan Delancey at the Eighth Precinct. He's handling the investigation into Sills's murder. He'll take care of you." She paused for a second, then dug a card and a pen out of her purse. "Here's one of my cards." She bent over the hall table and wrote rapidly. "This is Ethan's—Detective Delancey's name and number on the back."

Cristy shook her head. "I can't imagine a situation where I'd want to call a policeman, but thanks for the number." She looked at the card, then stuck it in the pocket of her robe. "I'll keep the card because it's got *your* number on it."

Chapter Ten

The police superintendent had finished his press conference and was taking questions when Ethan's phone vibrated. He'd told dispatch not to call him until the press conference was over. If this was the dispatcher, she was cutting it very close.

"Delancey," he said, stepping backward behind the curtains, away from the crowd of reporters and onlookers. The number on his screen wasn't familiar.

"Detective Delancey," the man said. "I'm Grayson Reed. D&D Securities. I was assigned to stake out this address for you." He read off Laney's address.

"That's right. What's the matter?"

"I've just handcuffed a woman who was breaking into the house. White female, mid-thirties, blonde—"

"What about Laney—Ms. Montgomery?"

"She isn't here. I've—"

"Not there? That's impossible. I had an officer—"

"Detective," Reed said with studied patience. "I've been here just over an hour, but until this person showed up there was no activity inside. The name on her driver's license is Carolyn Gertz. It's a Mississippi license, expired. Probably stolen or faked. I'm having her license plates run."

"Carolyn?" Ethan said. "We've been trying to locate her on a related matter. Where are you now?"

"I'm inside the house. I've called Dispatch to send a police cruiser for my detainee."

"What do you see there?" Ethan asked, terrified that something had happened to Laney before the security agent had gotten there. "Any sign of a struggle?"

"No. Also no purse or car keys. I did find a card on the foyer table that had the name of a local car dealership and the hours of its courtesy van. I believe—"

"Son of a—" Ethan started before he cut himself off. "She got a damn loaner car. Hell, she was gone before you got there."

"That's my conclusion, too," Reed said. "Here's the cruiser now. I'll follow it to the Eighth in my own vehicle and give my written report. Will you be there?"

"I can't say for sure. I may be pursuing a suspect of my own who's driving a dealer car," Ethan said. "I'll have someone waiting to take her into custody. Thanks." He hung up and rushed back to the station. He had to call the dealership and get the make and model and plates of the loaner car so he could track down his runaway victim.

But where had she gone? She had told him she'd wanted to go home and sleep, so why hadn't she done that? He sighed in frustration as he headed for his desk. Dixon was sitting there, absorbed in a report.

"You'll never believe what Laney did," he said, tossing his car keys onto the desk and flopping into the chair.

Dixon looked up. "Um, got a car from somewhere and went down to Meraux to see Cristal Mackey?"

Ethan stared at him. "It's Christine Mackey. Who told you about her?"

Dixon held up a smartphone in a white case. "That looks like—"

"Laney's phone," Dixon said. He slid it across the expanse of desk between them. "Take a look at the phone log."

Ethan pressed keys. "I already knew she got a loaner car. But how do you figure she knew about Cristal's real name and where she lived?"

"No idea, but the name and address are in her phone."

"Where was her phone anyhow?"

"It was under one of the chairs in the interview room where you were talking to her earlier."

Ethan slammed the phone down on the desktop. "That's what happened. She heard me talking to the officer who ran down Cristal Waters for me. Damn it. I should have been more careful." He stood and reached for his keys. "I've got to go," he said, just as his phone rang.

"Delancey," he growled.

"Detective, it's Holt, head of the lab. One

of my techs told me you were asking about a phone that had been bugged."

"Right, I was, but I'm in a hurry right now."

"Give me half a minute. He mentioned that you were leaving the bug in the phone so as not to tip off the hacker. Well, everything he told you that the bug can do is true, but there's more."

"More?" A tingle of apprehension started up Ethan's spine. "More what?"

"Some of these new bugs can activate the microphone on the bugged phone and display GPS locations even if the phone is off. Also, the hacker can see everything in the bugged phone's address book. If the hacker is online when the bugged person enters a new contact into the address book, the hacker can see it in real time."

Dread settled on Ethan's chest, heavy as lead. "Thanks. I've got an emergency." He hung up.

"Laney's in big trouble. Whoever bugged her phone knows where she is."

"Where is she?"

"In Meraux, going to see Christine Mackey. I've got to get out there. Call the sheriff of Meraux for backup, will you? Tell them to come in silent and give the deputy in charge my cell number so we can coordinate."

Dixon sat up, grabbing a pen and writing down what Ethan told him. "Sure thing. I'm on it."

"Wish me luck, Dixon. If I'm right, Sills's murderer is on Laney's tail.

LANEY GAVE CRISTY the card with Ethan's number on the back, hugged her and started for the door. But before she took three steps, the door crashed open with a loud, splintering sound.

Laney, gun-shy since Sills's murder, threw herself sideways, shouting, "Get down." She landed behind a table that sat just to the right of the front door. She pushed the table over to provide a bit of cover.

The first figure that burst in through the splintered door nearly stopped her heart. It was him. The man in black who had killed the senator and injured her. He was the same height, with the same long, lean form. He was standing in the same awkward position and brandishing what appeared to be a similar weapon. The only thing different was the mask. This time he wore a black and silver Mardi Gras mask that covered only the upper half of the face.

He hadn't noticed her yet, so she had a split second to examine the mask and the face. What she saw gave her a jolt.

Could she believe her eyes? She wasn't sure. She quickly assessed the black-encased body. The silhouette wasn't just lean, it was skinny. The tight black sweater and pants hinted at spare bones and sinewy muscles, the recognizable body type of a dedicated runner. Her gaze focused on the front of the sweater. Were those small, barely discernible breasts? And what was it about those shoes? She squinted. They were platform boots. High ones. No wonder the figure looked awkward.

The man in black was not a man at all. It was a woman.

In those few seconds while Laney's brain was working that out, the woman in the Mardi Gras mask moved into the room and backed against the wall, motioning for another black-clad figure to enter. This one was taller, larger, unmasked and—Laney did a double take—familiar. She'd seen the man before. But she couldn't remember where, and she didn't have time to rack her brain. She had to concentrate on staying alive, because now, Mardi Gras had spotted her.

But to Laney's surprise, she paid no attention to her. She gestured to the man. He walked over, grabbed Laney by the scruff of her neck and hauled her to her feet. He pushed her against the wall with more than a little force and pressed his forearm against her throat. "Don't give me any trouble, sister," he said.

Despite her terror, and despite the fact that the pressure on her throat was making it a little hard to breathe, Laney almost laughed at his fake *gangster* accent. She held up her hands. "No trouble here," she responded.

Mardi Gras's attention was on Cristy, who was standing in the center of the room. She pointed her weapon. "Okay, whore," she said in a smoky, booze and cigarettes voice. "I know you've got pictures of Sills. I want every shot of him—by himself and with other people." She paused for barely a second, in which Cristy didn't move.

"Did you hear me? I want those pictures—now!"

Laney's hand twitched to reach for the pocket of her jeans where she'd stuck the photos. Hopefully the corners weren't sticking out. And hopefully the man, who was over six feet tall and bulky, wouldn't search her.

"Stay still!" he growled, pressing his thick forearm harder into her neck.

"Oh—" she croaked, grabbing his arm with her fingers and digging her nails into his flesh. "Can't breathe."

He jerked backward, then pressed against her again. "Scratch me again and I'll cut your fingernails down to the knuckle."

Cristy had her hands up, palms out, and was telling Mardi Gras that she didn't know what photos she was talking about. "All the pictures I have are in that box," she said, gesturing with her head toward the box on the coffee table. "In fact, I was just looking at them this—"

"Don't even try to lie to me, you heathen," Mardi Gras said. She brandished the gun, but didn't move any closer to either Cristy or the box. "Put that ratty box in a bag."

"A bag?" Cristy repeated. "What kind of—"

"Shut up and do it! Trash bag, grocery bag. I don't care."

Cristy's face was colorless. She was as terrified as Laney herself was. As Cristy backed toward the kitchen area with her hands still up, Laney struggled against the big man's grip. She sucked in air audibly, exaggerating her difficulty breathing. "Please—" she choked out in a guttural whisper, then coughed.

"For goodness' sake, George, don't kill her yet!"

Laney coughed again and noticed that Cristy was moving steadily backward. She passed the island that separated the kitchen from the living room, and paused. After a second, Laney realized what she was doing. She was reaching inside a drawer.

Laney gasped. It was the drawer where she'd put her gun. Laney tried to shake her head, but Cristy had her eyes on Mardi Gras. All Laney got for her trouble was another thrust of the muscled forearm into her throat. She cried out wordlessly—almost soundlessly, and dug her nails into his flesh again.

With a growl, he flung her violently away from him. Her back slammed into the wall and she went down, the breath knocked out of her.

At that same instant Cristy took a sudden step to her left, which placed her behind the island. She ducked.

"Hey!" Mardi Gras shouted, taking a step forward.

Cristy raised her head, aimed her weapon and shot. The shot went wildly into the ceiling.

Mardi Gras shot back, splintering the corner of the island, then retreated and ducked behind the open front door. She leaned out and shot twice more.

Cristy rose up to fire back. The bullet went through the wooden door and Mardi Gras shrieked and cursed.

"Got you!" Cristy cried.

Get down, Laney tried to say but no sound came from her mouth. She clawed at the wall and scrabbled to regain her footing. The man pulled a gun and fired at Cristy.

Cristy cried out and went down.

"No!" Laney croaked, her voice barely audible. She got to her feet as the man waited, listening, and the woman kept cursing and calling Cristy names.

Sneaking between him and the table by the

door, Laney grabbed the narrow neck of the long copper vase and swung it with all her might, grunting with the effort. She had no idea if she had the strength to swing the heavy vase hard enough to bring him down.

He obviously heard her grunt, because he twisted toward her just as she followed through with her swing and hit him square in the temple. He went down like a rock.

Cristy cried, "Laney!" in a hoarse whisper.

Mardi Gras shouted, "George, finish her off, damn it. I'm bleeding like a stuck pig." She paused. "George!"

While the woman screamed, Laney was crawling over the downed man's bulk and reaching for his weapon. It was huge and heavy in her hands, but she lifted it and backed away from him, pointing it at the door behind which the woman cowered. "Cristy, are you all right?"

"Hit in the shoulder," Cristy gasped. "Can't use gun."

A harsh laugh erupted from behind the door. "Well, whore, it's what you deserve. George. Shoot her and let's get out of here."

Laney aimed the gun, holding it with both hands and sure she was going to drop it any minute. "George isn't available right now," she called out. "If you don't drop your gun and come out I'm going to shoot the door with his gun, and as big as it is, I'm thinking it just might blow a hole in the wood the size of—I don't know—*you*. On the count of three."

A shot echoed out and Laney heard wood splinter as a bullet zinged by her ear. The woman had blown a hole in the door she was hiding behind. Out of the corner of her eye, Laney saw the man stirring. Her arms were already becoming tired from holding the heavy gun straight out in front of her. She glanced at him, then at the splintered door as her mind raced.

Cristy was wounded, probably much worse than Mardi Gras, judging by their voices. George had been stunned for a while but now he was waking up. Laney had no idea what she was going to do now.

The big man lifted his upper body with his arms and shook his head, like a big cat or dog shaking off a nap.

"Don't move," Laney cried.

The man turned his head to look at her. She knew he saw her hands shaking with exhaustion from holding the gun up and out. He smiled, then laughed.

"Stop it!" she said. "Lie down flat."

Mardi Gras peeked out from behind the door. "Don't move, Elaine Montgomery," she said, "or I'll kill you."

Laney knew she was beat. She was no match

for the two of them. Her arm muscles were beginning to twitch with fatigue. And she was so worried about Cristy she could barely think. *Phone.*

"Cristy," she said. "Call the police."

"Oh, no you don't," George said, groaning as he worked to push himself to his feet.

"Don't move!" Laney shouted at him. "Do. Not. Move!"

"You don't move," Mardi Gras shouted.

And from somewhere, a third voice—a wonderfully familiar voice—said, "How about none of you move."

It was Ethan. Before Laney could even wonder how he'd found her, he and a roomful of officers rushed in. After that, everything deteriorated into chaos. At one point, Laney heard an officer reading the man his rights as he marched him out the door. Two men with bulletproof vests and rifles disarmed the woman in the Mardi Gras mask not two feet from where Laney was standing. When one of them yanked the mask off, the woman cursed at him.

Laney stared at the unmasked woman in shock and horror, scarcely able to believe what she was seeing. "It was you!" she said. "All the time, it was you." She was staring at Benita Davis, dressed all in black with platform boots and a mask. "You shot Senator Sills and me."

"Oh, shut up, you stupid—" the vulgar word Benita was about to say was cut off when one of the officers yanked on her arm to turn her toward the EMTs. "Ow!" she shrieked. "Police brutality! Help me! Call my lawyer. I demand my lawyer."

Laney opened her mouth, but a hard, firm hand grabbed her arm. She turned. It was Ethan.

"What did you just say?" he asked, frowning at her.

"I didn't say it," she responded. "I was going to but then I—"

"No. What did you say when you realized it was Benita behind that Mardi Gras mask?"

"Oh, Ethan. It's her. I mean it *was* her. She's the man in black. The one who killed Senator Sills and shot me. Look at her in that black sweater and pants. How skinny she is. How bony. It's her."

"But from the beginning you've said it was a man."

"I know. I thought it was. Being so skinny and—I mean, look. You can hardly see her breasts, and it was dark in that hotel room. But look at her," she gestured toward Benita. "She's skin and bone. And in those sky-high platform heels, she's almost as tall as I am."

Ethan shook his head. "That's not going to be easy to prove," he said. "All the reports, your witness statement, everything assumed the killer was a man. In fact, I was about con-vinced it was Buddy."

The EMTs had placed a protesting Benita on a stretcher and were carrying her out to the ambulance. Cristy had already been taken out. As soon as they loaded Benita in, the am-bulance would take them both to St. Bernard Parish Hospital for evaluation and treatment.

Around Laney and Ethan, people in crime scene jackets swarmed all over the apartment, taking fingerprints, marking small areas with numbered plaques and taking dozens and doz-ens of photographs. After a few minutes, Laney sat down on a small chair in the corner of the living room. Ethan stood beside her, as stoic as a palace guard. Dixon walked past them, call-ing out that he was following the ambulance to the hospital to try to talk to both Benita and Cristy.

A few minutes later, Officer Farrantino came

up to Ethan to ask him if he wanted her to take Laney to the station. He declined, saying he'd handle her. Slowly the house cleared out.

Laney waited, staring down at the hardwood floor. She knew that Ethan was standing over her, looking down at her. She didn't even raise her head.

Finally he spoke. "You want to tell me what the hell you thought you were doing?"

She didn't move. He was going to have to get it all out. All the anger, all the frustration, all the resentment he held for her. Once he did, she doubted there would be anything else inside him. Certainly nothing positive—nothing caring. She'd probably never see him acting as anything other than bad cop from now on.

"Laney, I'm talking to you."

She sighed, stared at a nail in a plank in the floor for a few more seconds, then looked up at him. "I know you are. I know you're angry and you have a right to be. There is no telling how many laws I've broken, and I'm prepared to face the consequences for that. I don't have an excuse. I wanted to see Cristal Mackey. I wanted to meet her for myself so I could find out what she knew about my father. Turns out she knew a lot—a whole lot that I didn't know. My father did pay blackmail to Senator Sills, but he didn't do it to protect himself. He paid it as protection for Cristal. For her to be able to take back her given name and to make a new life for herself. I knew my father was not bad."

"You knew—" Ethan stopped himself. He was so angry he felt sick. He knew he was on the verge of the kind of life-sucking, debilitating anger that his father had exhibited throughout his life. Anger that had always terrified him and his younger brother and sister growing up. Anger that had given his dad a stroke and confined him to a wheelchair.

Ethan had never wanted to experience that much rage. He'd spent his life convincing himself that he'd missed that gene. That he didn't have that anger inside him. But tonight, he found out that he did have that much rage inside him. And he found out what it took to bring it to the surface. Laney Montgomery. He took a deep breath. "You almost got Cristal and yourself killed. What the hell did you think you were going to do with that gun?"

Laney pushed herself to her feet, stifling a groan at the soreness in her back and hips from being slammed against the wall. "I took the gun after I knocked George out. Should I have left it there for him to pick up when he woke up?"

Ethan scowled at her. "You knocked him out?" he finally asked.

"With the copper vase. That one over there." She pointed. "I've already told you I'll take the consequences. I'll go to prison if I have to. But I can't be sorry I came here. I found Cristal and she gave me the information I needed. She gave me something else, too." She dug in the pocket of her jeans and pulled out two slightly wrinkled snapshots.

Ethan stared at them, first one, then the other, then the first one again and so on. He swallowed. He tried to speak but nothing would come out of his mouth.

"Where—" he croaked. "How—"

Laney just shrugged.

As the last two crime scene techs picked up their gear and walked out of the house, Ethan stared at Laney in undisguised shock.

"Do you know what this is?" he asked, holding the photos up.

She nodded. "Proof," she said tiredly.

Ethan shook his head slowly back and forth. "I'll be a son of a bitch," he muttered.

WHEN ETHAN STEPPED into the interview room at just after midnight, he found Laney sitting at the table with her head on her crossed arms on the table, asleep. He'd spent the past four, no, five, hours interrogating suspects. He'd started with George Firth, the Davises' chauffeur, who had shot Christine Mackey. George was only too happy to spill everything he knew in exchange for a plea deal. As it turned out, George and Benita had been lovers for years, and Benita had talked him into helping her frame Buddy, who was in the early stages of Alzheimer's, for the death of Darby Sills. Benita wanted the senator dead because she was sick of paying ever-increasing blackmail to him to keep him from exposing Buddy as, as she put it, a "whore-chasing son of a bitch." Benita had been sure that the silver belt buckle would prove that it was Buddy, and that the reason he'd worn it when he'd killed Sills was because he'd forgotten he'd had it on.

When Ethan got through with George, he had a pretty clear picture of Benita's means, motive and opportunity. She'd given Buddy a sleeping pill that night to ensure that he wouldn't wake up, then while she'd taken care of the senator at the hotel, she'd had George waiting outside to drive her back to the Circle of Faith compound and sneak in as if they'd never been gone.

Ethan tried to talk with Benita, but she demanded her lawyer and would not say another word. So he moved on to Carolyn, the woman Grayson Reed had brought in. She'd been carrying her own driver's license, so it was simple to identify her as Carolyn Gertz, Benita Davis's daughter from her first marriage. Benita had talked her into distracting Laney so George could sneak in and bug her phone.

Ethan sat down opposite Laney and rubbed

his face tiredly. Laney stirred, but didn't awaken. He knew she was exhausted. He was, too. But he had a job to do before either one of them could get any sleep.

Laney's mouth was slightly open and Ethan could hear her soft, even breaths. He watched her sleep. Every minute or so, she'd jerk slightly and make a distressed-sounding noise. He wondered if she were dreaming about the shootout in Cristal's apartment. Thinking about that made his scalp tighten with fear for her. It was a miracle that she hadn't been hit by a stray bullet. He pushed a strand of hair back from her temple where it was threatening to fall over her face, brushing the backs of his fingers across her soft skin.

She opened her eyes.

He jerked his hand away.

"Oh," she said drowsily, lifting her head but

leaving her eyes closed. "Sorry. I didn't mean to fall asleep. I just—"

He stood, backing away and leaning against the wall, hoping he looked a hell of a lot more relaxed than he felt. His unease was not only from interviewing reluctant—and in Benita's case, hostile—suspects. It wasn't only from being so angry at Laney for putting herself in such terrible danger. It was also that when he'd seen her asleep with her head in her arms, he'd been hit with a poignant ache in the middle of his chest. It was painful and sweet at the same time, and he didn't like it.

He didn't want to feel pulled in two different directions when he looked at her. He didn't want to care that she was exhausted, or worry that she might be ill or injured. He didn't want to realize that the only way he could be happy and content was if she was happy and content. He huffed in frustration.

She forced herself to open her eyes, squinting at the bright light in the room. "Look, Ethan, I'm sorry—" she started.

"You're *sorry?*" he mimicked. "Really? Well, that's just great. That wipes away everything you did." Wincing, he tried to ask himself what the hell he thought he was doing, being mean to her after all she'd been through. He realized he had no answer. He didn't know why. All he knew was that he was furious with her for putting herself in harm's way.

"I know it doesn't. I just—"

He sliced his hand through the air like a saber, cutting her off. "Damn straight it doesn't. You ignored me, you ran away from a protected house where I'd placed a bodyguard to keep you safe. You took information from an ongoing investigation—" he stopped and stared at her. "You eavesdropped on an official police conversation."

Laney ducked her head. "I could hear both sides of the conversation," she said meekly.

That was his fault. "I should have been more careful, but," he said, shaking his head. "I've got to tell you, I'd have thought you had more sense than that."

"I didn't mean to cause problems. I just wanted to know if she knew my dad and what she could tell me about him." She paused for a second before continuing. "Do you have any idea what it's like to find out that the father you trusted, that you worshiped, went to prostitutes, did things that made him vulnerable to blackmail, lied to you? Do you know what it's like to learn, within the space of a couple of days, that you never really knew your father at all?"

"You're not alone in how you feel, Laney. I think every adult eventually realizes their parents are just people, not saints and not superheroes. The difference is how you deal with it."

He drew in a frustrated breath. "And the way you dealt with it was to go running off like a—a kid with no sense of responsibility, and get a woman shot."

"How do you figure that I got her shot?" she demanded. "Benita had no idea I was there."

"Oh, yeah? Well, would it surprise you to know that when you typed Cristal's address into your phone, the information transferred immediately to Benita's chauffeur, the guy who bugged your phone?"

"Oh, my God. The phone can do that?" Laney paused. "That means it's my fault they knew where she was." Her face crumpled.

"That's right. Cristal had taken back her real name, so Benita had never been able to find her. Buddy had told her that Cristal had pictures. She didn't know you were there. She went to Cristal's house to get the photos. Not to protect Buddy. Benita wanted to plant them so they implicated Buddy and helped prove that he wanted Sills dead."

"She wanted to implicate Buddy? I thought they were inseparable. Why?"

"Apparently Buddy is in the beginning stages of Alzheimer's. He's forgetting things, getting confused. According to her chauffeur, who's turning state's witness, she had this big plan to kill Sills to stop the blackmail and frame Buddy for it. Then she'd take over the Circle of Faith ministries and she and George, the chauffeur/lover/computer hacker, could live happily ever after. It almost worked, too. If she'd managed to kill Cristal and get out of there with the incriminating photographs, she might have succeeded."

Laney was staring at her hands. "It was my fault Cristy was shot." She looked up at him. "I've messed up everything, haven't I?"

Ethan shrugged. "No," he said with a little

smile. "You didn't screw up everything. You did get the photos. And believe me. It was only a matter of time before Benita and George found her. So actually, by leading them there while you were there to help her, you saved her life."

Laney nodded, pushing her fingers through her hair. "How is she doing? Cristy, I mean."

"Last I heard she was doing fine. The bullet went through her shoulder without hitting the bone, so she's got a nice entrance and exit wound, but no serious damage."

"That's good." Laney took a long breath. "So do you need me for anything else?"

Ethan wondered how he was supposed to answer that question. He looked at her for a long time.

"Ethan?"

"No," he said. "You're free to go."

She stood with a sigh and slid past him to the door and turned the knob. "Ethan?"

He turned. "Yeah?"

"I'm glad I got to know you," she said.

His heart felt as though it had dropped to his toes. "Me, too," he said. "But we'll be seeing each other again."

"We will?"

His head snapped up. Had she sounded hopeful? He studied her face, but all he saw was pale exhaustion. It was all he could do to keep his expression neutral. "Yeah. I'll need to get you to sign your statement and you'll probably have to testify about the photos and about your father's finances, whenever this comes to trial."

"How—how long do you think that will be?"

"Could be as long as several years. It depends on how good Benita's lawyers are, and whether George sticks to his plea agreement."

She nodded. "So I guess I'll hear from you?"

Ethan looked at her long and hard, then stepped up closer to her. "I could have someone else get in touch with you."

She blinked. "Okay, if—if that's what you want."

"I don't," he said. "Laney?"

She swallowed. "Yes?"

"I don't want you—" His mouth went dry.

Her brows furrowed.

"I don't want you to—" He swallowed and tried again. "I don't want you to leave."

"You don't?"

"You're the most annoying, most stubborn and most fascinating person I've ever met in my life."

"Thank you…" she said cautiously.

He smiled. "I'm sure you probably feel the same about me."

"You are stubborn," she said. "And pigheaded and officious and arrogant and—"

He bent his head and kissed her, hard and long. When he finally lifted his head they were both out of breath.

"And—" she took a breath "—confusing and irritating and—"

"I'll do it again," he warned.

"Oh, no," she said, smiling. "How long will I have to endure this?"

"Well," he said, touching the corner of her lip with his thumb. When he did, she closed her eyes and sighed. "We do have to put up with each other until this trial is over. It could be years and years—and years."

"Promise?" she asked, lifting her head and kissing him on the lips.

"I promise," he answered, pulling her close. "And here's another promise. Once this trial is over, I'll make you a big pot of spinach pasta and we can see what comes up in the conversation."

Laney laughed and put her arms around Ethan's neck. "I'll hold you to that promise."

* * * * *